A collection c

cookies.

Peanut Blossoms and the Matchmaking Kitten by Claire Davon

Red Velvet Crinkles and Christmas Sprinkles by Maria Imbalzano

Tinsel and Tea Cakes by Jill Piscitello

Stirred with Peppermint

by

Claire Davon
Maria Imbalzano
Jill Piscitello

Stirred with Peppermint

The Wild Rose Press, Inc.
PO Box 708
Adams Basin, NY 14410-0708
Visit us at www.thewildrosepress.com

Publishing History
First Edition, 2022
Trade Paperback ISBN 978-1-5092-4497-3

Published in the United States of America

Peanut Blossoms and the Matchmaking Kitten

by

Claire Davon

Christmas Cookies Series

Dedication

Thank you to all the rescue kitties and animal rescuers who have graced my life over the years!

Meow.

The plaintive wail startled me. I glanced around my one-bedroom apartment. My TV was off, and the radio was playing classical at a volume acceptable for this time before sunrise. Nothing stirred in the building except me.

Meow.

I couldn't pinpoint where the sound was coming from. I lived alone, so no roommate had smuggled a cat inside. Unless I missed a cat in my grocery shopping yesterday, none had come home with me.

Maybe it was someone else's TV, but I didn't often hear my neighbors before dawn. I took a sip of coffee, trying to wake up so I could begin my day.

The peaceful hours before Portland came awake were my favorite time of day. This was the first time I'd been on my own in the entirety of my twenty-five years, and I was glorying in that fact. Nobody could tell me when to do things—except I had to be considerate of my fellow apartment dwellers.

I would start baking when it was light. Nothing could take the place of a still-warm cookie fresh from the oven melting over my tongue. Just the thought of it made my mouth water. *Soon*, I promised the ingredients waiting to be assembled.

Meow.

I was on the second floor, so it couldn't have been a cat that wandered in off the street. I set my coffee down and checked the tiny apartment just in case. No cat in the bedroom. No cat in the closet.

Meow. Meow! Maybe I was hearing a cat through the vents? They did allow pets in this building, with a deposit, so it was possible. The complex was built at right angles, and the acoustics could be strange.

I went to the sliding door that led to my itty-bitty balcony. It was little more than a slab of concrete with a wrought iron fence more decorative than functional. Nope. No cat on the balcony—thank goodness. The temperature was too cold for felines.

Meow. Meow!

It sounded like it was coming from the front door. How could a cat have gotten up to the second floor? Not through the elevator, unless it was the sort of feline capable of pressing buttons.

As I got closer, the scrabbling of claws told me I had been right. I yanked the door open.

A gray-and-white kitten, maybe three months old, was pawing at the wood. I stared at the short-haired fur ball, and he looked back at me with an expectant gaze. I knelt and held out my hand.

"Hi there, little guy. How did you get there?"

Meow. He nosed my hand and then butted it.

"Where did you come from?" I picked him up, hoping he wouldn't slash at me with his kitten claws. His small body was warm in my hands. He didn't fight me when I carried him inside. His ease with my touch suggested he wasn't feral.

He nuzzled me, a purr starting like the rumble of an engine. My parents had animals over the years, but I hadn't been able to get one. My last roommate was allergic. Maybe when I started my new job and was more settled in. I was lucky—I knew that. Entry level finance positions may not be everyone's idea of glamour, but the unexpected offer halfway across the country was a chance I'd had to seize. I'd grabbed the first apartment I could rather than risk losing it, which meant a move at the end of the year and no money to return home. I'd be fine, as soon as I got through the holidays.

The cat let out a small hiss when I drew up his tail to determine sex—male. His coat wasn't shiny, but it wasn't dirty either. His medium-length fur was half-combed, and he wasn't scratching like he had parasites. He was an enigma wrapped in fur.

I went to the refrigerator and took out leftover hamburger from the night before. When I heated it up, the kitty meowed. After I set it down, he began devouring it at once.

"You're quite the mystery." I doubted he'd been left at my door as a prank—I didn't know anyone in this new city who would do such a thing.

The cat had a few streaks of what appeared to be grease along his side and tail, but he wasn't filthy. Dirt still lingered on his skin, but he was free of fleas.

If nobody claimed him, I'd put up signs. I ticked off the things I would need if he hung around. A litter box. Wet food. Toys. The last thing I had in mind was going shopping on Christmas Eve, but I might have to.

"Well, kitty, I don't know who you are or how you got here, but welcome to Casa de Oriane. I'm going to make some cookies. Want to help?"

The cat said nothing as he continued to ravage the remnants of the hamburger patty. I took that for agreement and pulled out ingredients to start what the kitten had delayed.

The secret to good cookie making was in the mise

en place. That's what the cooking channels told me. I got out bowls and located the recipe bookmarked on my tablet.

I tried not to think about my family across the country or the fact that I had no plans for Christmas. When I'd made the choice to take the new job a month ago, moving in December had seemed reasonable. Now I was on the cusp of a holiday with nobody to share it with.

I was halfway through my task when I heard footsteps in the hallway. I expected the unknown person to keep on going. Instead, they stopped in front of my door. I went still. One of my neighbors could be a sociopath. I was glad for the chain and the double locks.

Meow.

The gray-and-white cat rubbed against my leg and then tried to climb up it. His sharp claws dug into my calf. I bent down to remove him from my flesh at the same time someone knocked on my door.

"Who is it?" I scooped up the kitty, then tucked him in the crook of my elbow as I went to the door.

I peered through the peephole, and my breath caught. Standing outside my door was a delicious hunk of man. He had a tousled, distracted air and was sweaty. His sweatpants and sneakers suggested he had been running. I hadn't heard him leave, but the apartments that direction were near a back staircase.

"It's Jet. Your neighbor. Sorry to be a bother. Your light is on, so I'm hoping I didn't wake you. I'm looking for a cat. Did you see one by any chance?"

Good-looking men made great criminals. "Describe the cat."

His smile even through the distortion of the

peephole could have lit a hundred women on fire. "The rascal is gray and white. Got a purr like a freight train and a bit of grease on his tail from where he was stuck in the truck engine."

Trusting strangers was how people died. "How do I know you're my neighbor?" The cat wriggled, and I let him jump down. He scurried to the kitchen and tried to leap onto the counter but missed. He bounced and then straightened, shaking his body before he started grooming himself.

"I reckon you're right. Can't be too careful. Back in a jiffy."

I glanced at the cat as his footsteps retreated and then returned.

"Here." Something slid under my door. A driver's license. It bore an awful picture of the man I had seen in the peephole and identified him as Jethro Tallans, resident of my apartment complex.

"I guess you are who you say you are." I reached for a spoon anyway, just in case.

"Yes, ma'am. Have you seen my cat?"

I kept the spoon at the ready and opened the door.

The kitty paid him no attention when Jethro stepped inside, but I did. All my senses roared to life at the incredible, six-foot-two specimen of man. His hair was brown with streaks of red, and his eyes were the kind of color people called hazel. He had a marvelous body with wide shoulders that begged to be leaned on. His legs…well…I could imagine them on mine.

I stared at him for a beat too long. A smile tugged at Jethro's lips. He held out his hand for his license. I handed it back to him, heat prickling my cheeks in the quiet.

"Jet?"

"My uncle is named Jethro. I don't cotton to the name. Been Jet all my life."

He had a faint twang that placed him somewhere down south, but I didn't know a Texas accent from a Louisiana one. I'd been told they were different.

"Hi, Jet." I put the spoon down and offered him my hand. "I'm Oriane. Is this your kitten?"

The kitty meowed and clawed at my ankle. I swooped down to grab him. Jet held his hands out for the cat, and I returned him to his owner.

"Yes, ma'am. This rascal's mine, at least for now." He gave the kitten a scratch, and the loud purr that accompanied the caress rumbled through its small body. "Two days ago, I was at the mall, and I heard meowing. He must have crawled into the pickup's engine and fell asleep there. Guy who owned the truck barely gave me time to get him out. He blazed out of there as soon as I freed the scamp."

Good-looking and he rescued animals. I had to fight to keep from swooning right then and there.

"How did he get into the hallway?"

Jet gave a rueful, lopsided grin that just about had me turning to mush.

"He must have slipped outside when I was fixin' to go on my run." He gestured toward my front door. "Scared me to death when I came home and couldn't find him." His relieved smile said he was telling the truth.

"I'm glad he's okay. You've got an escape artist on your hands."

"I know."

"What are you naming him?" I doubted he would keep the kitten, but maybe he would find it a good home.

"I should call him hellion, but I'm thinking Buster. I have a feeling he's going to be busting a lot of things."

We were winding down on small talk, and I had to let him make a graceful exit. Even though I didn't want to.

"Buster. You're one lucky cat, Buster. Jet, it was nice to meet you. I should let you get this crazy feline back to your place."

He gestured to the cookie makings on my counter. "And I'll let you get back to whatever tasty treat you have there. Nice to meet you, neighbor. Oriane. You know where to come if you need to borrow a cup of sugar." His eyes twinkled, and it was all I could do to keep from passing out.

"I suppose I do."

****

Meow. Meow, meow.

I pulled open the front door, and Buster darted in. I closed the door after the kitten, who began rubbing against my leg.

"You are a little demon, aren't you?" I'd noted the soft tread of footsteps on the stairs about ten minutes ago, sounds I'd never been aware of before.

Buster started purring. I picked him up, and he snuggled into my hand.

"Is someone looking for you, sweetie? Someone besides Jet? You're awfully affectionate for a stray. Did you get out and take a ride somewhere you shouldn't, and people are missing you?"

He licked my hand and stared at me with big eyes that would rival the movie version of *Puss in Boots* for their cuteness.

Almost as cute as the man who had taken this kitten

on.

My peanut blossom cookies were baked and ready for…I didn't know what. I'd made them out of habit and still had enough for a second batch. Maybe I could give some to my neighbor. I could borrow that cup of sugar he offered.

He was going to have to come and fetch his cat. With that in mind I carried Buster with me to the bedroom to select more appropriate clothing than my slouchy sweats. I decided to look casual and not like I was prepared for him to come over. No makeup for sure, but I would brush my hair. I set the kitten down and selected the Christmas pajamas my parents had sent me. No, maybe I shouldn't wear jammies. Maybe I should. Jeggings would be better. And a nice shirt, but not too obvious. I decided on a blue tunic that brought out the color of my eyes.

Clothes changed and hair brushed, I retreated back to the living room. After what seemed like an eternity but was fifteen minutes at most, a knock sounded on my door.

"Sorry to interrupt, ma'am," Jet said when I opened the door. "Is…?" He broke off when I handed him Buster as he stepped inside.

I closed the door and faced him. *Ma'am?* "That kitten has a mind of his own."

Jet sighed and tapped Buster on the nose. "You have to stop that before it all goes cattywampus. You'll have my pretty neighbor thinking I'm a plumb bad cat dad."

Pretty neighbor? I could deal with that. "There's a neighbor between your apartment and mine. I'm surprised he didn't go there."

Jet grinned at me, and my heart flipped over.

"Mister Gabard smells like stale Old Spice and cigarettes. Buster has better taste than that."

I hadn't met Mister Gabard, so I'd have to take him at his word.

"I sure am sorry about this. He keeps escaping. I'm glad I live on the second floor and have such a sweet neighbor. I'd be pitching a fit if he got out and something happened to him."

I stood there, unsure of what to say, caught between inviting him for coffee and knowing that I had no business doing anything of the sort. "There are tricks to keeping them in. You can lock him in another room before you go out, or slide your foot in the doorway as you open it so he can't get out."

He raised an eyebrow. "It sounds like you been around the block a time or two with cats."

"We had them growing up. I learned how to poke my grocery bag through the front door so our escape-artist cat didn't bolt outside. I can show you a few tricks if you like." Why had I said that? He was far too cute and charming to be single.

"I'd sure appreciate it. None of my pals have cats, and the rescue groups are busy for the holidays."

Darn. If he was contacting rescues, that meant he was trying to give the kitten away. My opinion of him faltered.

"You don't want to keep him? I know it requires a pet deposit, but other people have animals, so…" I let the sentence trail off, disappointment gripping me.

Buster meowed and pushed on Jet's forearms with his paws. "Is it all right with you if I set him down?"

I nodded, retreating a step into the tiny living room. Buster jumped down and attacked a nearby shoelace.

Damn it. I'd forgotten to put those sneakers away. My whole place was a mess.

"I've posted a notice on the local neighborhood website, but nobody has come forward. If they don't, then I reckon he's mine. My friends are telling me not to. I've got an active lifestyle, and a pet might infringe on that."

Of course he did. He was far too gorgeous and charming not to have women throwing themselves at him.

"But he's cute as the dickens, and I found him. That means I'm responsible for him. Besides, the rescue groups have other things to do than worry about a kitten who's got a good place to stay. Nah, I'm fixin' to make him mine if nobody turns up. I had questions, though, and figured they could answer them."

I turned a relieved smile on him, my good will restored. "Did they? Have ideas?"

"Someone is going to get back to me. They get a lot of emails, I'm sure."

"Yeah." I turned away and then laughed when Buster bounded into the living room, stalking my vertical blinds. "He's a bit of a monster, isn't he? Would you like some coffee?"

He shook his head. "I'm as busy as a cat on a hot tin roof and need to get to it. I'll take one of those cookies if that's all right."

I cast a gaze at the wrapped pile. "Sure. I don't know what I'm going to do with them anyway." I stopped before I could make myself sound any more pathetic than I already was.

He raised an eyebrow. "You baked them with no plans on what to do with them? Were you going to eat them all yourself?"

I flushed and turned my gaze away. My hips could use a little work, sure, but I was okay with my body. "It's habit. I love to bake. I have enough for a second round too."

His grin was so infectious I forgot my pique about the suggestion that I might be overweight.

"I know a place they can go to good use. I've got Christmas Eve plans with friends. It's nothing fancy." He cocked his head toward the plate. "Why don't you come with me? You'd be welcome, especially if you come with those."

I shook my head. "We've just met. Your friends don't want a stranger at Christmas."

Buster took the opportunity to jump on my foot, and I squealed when his needle-sharp claws pierced my bare flesh. Jet reached down and scooped him up, and the kitten hissed, his mouth opening and closing before he started purring.

"Ouch. Buster." I glanced down to see if he'd caused major damage but couldn't see blood. "Be careful."

Jet seemed unperturbed by the tiny needles piercing his flesh. "We had barn cats growing up but none that got domesticated."

I made my snap decision. It was foolish—he was a stranger—but I didn't have anywhere else to go for Christmas. "Well, if you want the company," I said, pretending like I was doing him a favor, instead of the reverse, "I'll join you. If you're sure your buddies won't mind."

He ducked his head, and that shy gesture made my heart flip over. I could see him on the big screen, lighting up women's hearts. Or just mine.

"I'll fetch you around four. If you've got an ugly sweater, wear it. We have a contest."

"Do you think Buster will be okay by himself?"

"If he can travel in a pickup and not get carved up, he can spend a few hours alone. I got him a bunch of toys and plenty of food. I'll lock him in the bathroom, although I'm sure he'll be mad as a wet hen about that. Otherwise, he might find a way to get out again."

I shuddered at the idea of the little guy getting caught in the engine. That this kitten nearly died because he was trying to get warm was appalling. Even knowing it happened far too often didn't stop me from wanting to cuddle Buster against the tragedy of life.

"He already lost one of his nine lives. I'll be ready. When you say around four, do you mean four o'clock on the dot or just thereabouts?"

He grinned, and that dratted heart of mine soared.

"Got it. You throw a hissy if people are late?"

I shrugged, toeing the edge of the rug with my bare foot. Buster wiggled his rear, and I stopped moving my foot. He stared at it and then started licking his paw.

"I like to know when I'm expected."

"Then I'll make sure I'm not late, else you'll eat all the cookies."

"Got that right."

****

I don't know what possessed me to wear my sweater with the tree appliques and the lights, but when Jet beamed at me, I decided I'd made the right choice. Another guy might have thought it nerdy, but from the little I knew about Jet, I thought he would appreciate the spirit. He'd said an ugly sweater, but many people would take that to mean something form fitting in red or green.

Mine draped over my shoulders and hung down like a box. It was by far the ugliest one I had.

The sight of him in jeans and a holiday sweatshirt almost stopped my heart. In sweats he was a bit of a casual mess. Groomed and with tight denim showing off his legs, he was almost too much to bear.

I gestured for him to lead the way.

He took my hand and tucked it into his elbow as if it were the most natural thing to do. He smiled, and it was so breathtaking I just stared. I had to get my hormones under control.

"You're a sight, all right. That's one ugly sweater. You should win the contest."

I already had.

I couldn't be mooning over him like this. He was just being nice, and I was ridiculous. He took in stray cats. He might have a habit of collecting those in need. I was just another project. He saw "neighbor alone for Christmas," and his rescue instincts swung into action.

A woman with a snug green sweater and well-applied makeup answered the door with a smile of welcome.

One that increased when she saw Jet…and fell when she saw me.

"Hi, Jet, come on in. You're just in time. We're about to start the games. Who's this?"

I fumbled for the cookies and held them out to her. She sniffed at my offering and didn't move.

"Gail, this is my neighbor Oriane. She had nowhere to go at Christmas, so I invited her along. Oriane, this is my friend Gail."

Friend. Not that I had any claim on him.

Gail smacked him on the arm, her hand lingering on

his skin. She waved us inside, and we headed toward the open-plan kitchen to the right of the front door. It had a designer touch with its middle island and gleaming vent hood. Several dishes and a bucket of chicken were on the counter, looking incongruous next to expensive dinnerware.

"You and your strays. How is that little beast you rescued anyway? Have you called the shelter yet?"

I disliked her for those comments. For those comments—and those alone.

Sure.

She nudged him. "I'm kidding, but he was quite a sight when you first got him." She looked over at me, and her smile was cool and unwelcoming. "I was with him when he got the kitten out of the engine. He got oil on my car seats."

"Buster is not a mess anymore." I had no business caring if he was dating this woman or not. They fit together, with her dark good looks and well-proportioned body. She had the perfect amount of makeup, and her house reflected what I assumed was an interior designer's flair.

"Buster. You named it." Gail sniffed and then gestured toward the counter for me to set the cookies down.

"Gail was helping me with my shopping," Jet said. "Good thing too or that little fella was a goner. We were in the right place at the right time."

"Yes. Lucky us. Thank you for paying for the car wash."

My impression of Jet slid a little by this friend of his who wanted to be more than that. He introduced me to the four other people who were there, all friends of a few years' time, correlating to when Jet arrived in Portland.

I was greeted by a hail of welcomes as we emerged into the living room where more designer styles awaited. Her couch, where two men were lounging, looked more form than function in an off-white. The matching armchairs faced inward. A faux fire burned in a fireplace that had no chimney.

Gail claimed Jet, sitting near him on the sofa and relegating me to one of the chairs. She leaned over to say something to him, and her hand lingered on his arm.

"How do you guys know one another?" I took a sip of my wine. I couldn't afford to drink too much. I would make an idiot of myself if I did so.

Wayne, the largest and most boisterous of the men, poked a finger at Jet. "We did a turn selling hot dogs at Ducks games when Jet first got here. Then I got a real gig but kept in touch with Jet. The rest of us know each other through work. Boring office job, but it pays the bills."

"I didn't stay there long." Gail tapped Jet with manicured fingernails.

Her toiletry bill could have sent me home for Christmas. I fought down my dislike. I was being catty and had no place to be jealous. I was the interloper, not her.

"I work for Nike. It's a much better gig. I keep telling Jet he should stop with the part-time temp jobs and come work with us. I could get him a job. He's got that math degree, after all. If he went for his CPA or MBA, he'd be set for life."

I raised my eyebrow at Jet. Math degree?

He shook his head. "That dog don't hunt, Gail. What I'm doing suits me. When I figure out what I want to do,

I'll change it."

"Yes, but if you had a better job, you could move out of that…hovel." Her gaze slid to me, and I looked away.

"The apartment building is fine. Not all of us are lucky enough to have our grandparents' place as an option."

Score one for Jet.

Gail's sour look hinted she didn't like being corrected. "Whatever you say."

Wayne burped and grinned at the assembly. "What goes in must come out."

Him I liked. He had a temperament that suggested he covered his feelings with loud gestures. I knew insecurity when I saw it. Just as I knew predators when I saw them.

"You're gross, Wayne."

His grin widened. "You know you love me."

Then we moved to the Christmas sweater competition where we were forced to model our sweaters. I was conscious of the bulky knit of mine compared to Gail's glittering, green confection. She looked perfect. She sipped from her wine glass and cast glances toward Jet. He didn't seem to notice.

Staying home would have been better. I was enjoying their company, but Gail's side-eyes were starting to wear me down. I could leave, get in an Uber, and head home.

That would be rude. I didn't fight with mean girls and let them have the field to themselves, but I knew one when I saw one.

Wayne took the slips of paper from the people and marked them down one by one. He gave me and Gail a smile. "You guys got all the votes. The winner is…Oriane!"

I gaped, and Gail gagged on her wine.

"Oriane? The newcomer?" She spat my name out, her mouth twisting.

Wayne handed me a small box that wound up containing an ugly-sweater pin. I glanced at Jet who took it and put it on my sweater without being asked.

"Yours is nice, Gail, but it's too pretty. Oriane's is a sight with that garland and balls."

Gail's sharp look missed nothing. "Yes, it's very retro. I can't believe your latest orphan project's Christmas sweater won over mine. Where did you buy it, Goodwill?"

I opened my mouth to answer the question, but Jet got to his feet, breaking off whatever I was going to say.

"Quit being ugly. Appreciate the hospitality, Gail, but we're leaving." He held out his hand to me, and I took it in a daze.

"Come on now," Gail said, getting to her feet as well.

The others retreated, Wayne making a theatrical gesture of shock.

"I was just kidding. It's a joke. You can take a joke, can't you, Oriane? You have a sense of humor to buy that sweater."

I was going to say something, but Jet tugged on my hand, and I stayed quiet. Wayne belched in an obvious move to defuse the tension, but Jet ignored him.

"Oriane, get your tin. I'll say my goodbyes."

"Jet, that's not necessary."

"Yes, it is. You're here as my guest. There's no call for insults."

"You're overreacting," Gail said, sputtering the words. "You're ruining Christmas. If I said something to offend, then I apologize. Just sit down, and we'll pretend this didn't happen." She grabbed at his hands, but he stepped away.

"Hush your mouth. It wasn't me who ruined it."

"It's your fault we're having our celebration today instead of tomorrow. You and that shelter you volunteer at. Goodness gracious, Jet, lots of people help the homeless this time of year. You don't have to."

If he backed down, I would stay. I might have a good time if Gail stopped being a cow. His friends seemed like fun folks. She had to have her good points for Jet to associate with her.

"Yes, I do." He went into the kitchen and came out with my half-empty tin, which he handed to me. It was a small detail, but it told me how different he was than all other guys I'd met. Most wouldn't even notice. A container and a handful of peanut blossom cookies would have been a worthy sacrifice in the battle of Jet standing up for me.

"Stop. Just stop. We were having fun. Don't let her spoil things." Gail's glare at me could have sizzled a glacier into puddles.

"Ain't gonna destroy my Christmas." He glared at Gail before waving a hand to the others. "Merry Christmas, all."

****

When we got to my apartment, he hesitated and then gestured down the hall toward his. "Want to come to my place? I've got brandy, and I'm sure Buster would love the attention. We shouldn't end the night on that note."

I should decline. Gail's nasty words slid through my

mind, a reminder that I didn't know what made this man tick. I warred with my two sides for a moment and then nodded. It was Christmas. I could indulge myself. "Sure. I'd love to see Buster. I'll come in for a few minutes."

He gestured to the remnants of my stupid offering. "I could use another one of those, though they might not go with brandy."

I grimaced at the anticipated taste of the two together but summoned a smile. "I guess we'll find out." Gail had been a witch, but that wasn't his fault. I might have been too if the guy I liked showed up with a stray in tow. I had to admit the sparks of jealousy that went through me when I was first introduced to Gail. I was no better than she was—I was just on the right end of his attentions.

Pathetic meows could be heard through the closed bathroom door as we entered, followed by a banging.

Jet glanced toward the door and then at me. "I'll warm the brandy if you let him out." He plucked the container from me.

The layout of his apartment was the same as mine, except flipped ninety degrees. The minute I opened the door, Buster sprang out and began meowing for my attention. I picked him up and scratched his head, marveling at the one-cat wrecking crew he was. Toilet paper was strewn around as though he'd gotten on top of the roll and unraveled it. A razor lay on the floor, and a shampoo bottle had been knocked over in the shower stall.

"Um…he destroyed things in here."

A groan from the kitchen was so long and heartfelt that I smiled. The miasma of earlier lifted from the chaos of one tiny kitten.

"Dang it! I forgot to put the toilet paper away. Is there any left, or did he shred it all?"

I stared at the mess as Buster nestled into me, purring. Shards of white were scattered on the ground like confetti. "Shredded. You might be able to salvage some."

"Would you see your way to hiding the remains in the cabinet? Buster, we had this conversation."

Buster purred, his eyes closed and his mouth open in a pose of extreme contentment. He did not look like the wretch that had destroyed an entire roll. I scratched under his chin, and the purr increased.

I came back into the living room with the cat in the crook of my arm. Jet had a Christmas tree that he'd anchored to the ceiling with a hook. The ornaments on the first branches were nonbreakable ones. I wondered if he'd had a few casualties along the way.

"Done. Your TP is safe from marauders." His apartment was clean and relatively neat.

He came out of the kitchen area with a tray that had the remaining cookies and two glasses of brandy. If they weren't in proper snifters, I could forgive him for that. If anything, it was another endearing thing about him.

I bet Gail was blowing up his phone, but he showed no interest in flipping it over to check.

Second-hand Christmas sweater. Ruined Christmas.

Buster meowed, and I set him down. He went bounding across the floor and careened into Jet, who was balancing the tray as he walked toward me. I almost laughed at the man dodging a two-pound fluff ball, but instead my breath caught.

This was a mistake. I should go back to my apartment.

I sat on the sofa and placed my arms on my legs. I was aware of my Christmas sweater, the one Gail had so derided, and wished I'd stopped to change. I had a cute pink sweater that drew attention to my figure. I should have worn that one in the first place.

When Jet sat down, Buster dug his claws into the sofa to get to where we were. Jet laughed and plucked him from the arm and put him on the cushions.

"He'll leave fur on it and holes."

He shrugged. "Nothing in this apartment is very expensive. I don't give a darn. Furniture can be replaced. Here." He slid the tray toward me. "Take a 'snifter' and a cookie."

"Only the best." I took the glass and snagged a cookie. The tip of the chocolate kiss had broken off, and cracks in the sugar showed where I'd pressed too hard. Not my finest effort, but it would taste good just the same.

"Only the best," he repeated, meeting my eyes.

He took a sip, and I followed. The brandy slid down my throat and warmed me from the inside, taking away some of the chill from the unpleasant events such a short time ago.

He cleared his throat, his lips turned down. "Oriane, I sure am sorry about what happened tonight. I invited you to enjoy a Christmas Eve with friends, and instead you got piled on. I would never have brought you if I'd known that was going to happen."

"It wasn't your fault." The sting of Gail's barbs was still buried in my flesh, but I wouldn't admit that to him. "She…" How did I ask if she had a claim?

"It wasn't her fault either," he said, and my heart quivered.

21

He was defending her. *Ugh*. Even though we left, he might have done it to teach her a lesson in manners. For all I knew, they would be talking again before morning, the rough edges smoothed out.

He held up a hand when I opened my mouth to speak. "She had no right to go for you like that. She owes you an apology. But to be fair to her, I've never come out and said I wasn't interested in dating her. I thought time would take care of that for me, but I should have been clearer. Being quiet about my feelings gave her false hope. I'm sorry."

He was apologizing to me? To cover my confusion, I took another sip and a nibble. "It's okay," I mumbled, the delicious cookie tasting like sand.

Buster took that moment to pounce on my hand.

Jet barked out a laugh. "I'm fixin' to go to the shelter tomorrow. You're welcome to come with me if you have no plans. I promise nobody will be there who will criticize your sweater. Which is cute as a bug, by the way."

I shouldn't be so vulnerable to a few sweet words. But on this Christmas Eve, removed from all I knew, the kindness pierced me.

"I'll come. Should I make that second batch of cookies? I would welcome an assistant." Not that I needed his help, but doing it together would be fun, just like Christmases back home.

"I'm guessing that means me because Buster doesn't have opposable thumbs. What time? Nine good? I have to be at the shelter at eleven. Does that leave us enough time? Or is eight better?"

How about five? Or how about you come over, and then you'll be there in the morning?

"Eight might be better," I mumbled and rose. Buster meowed at me, and I gave him a scratch. "I should go. It's late."

"Yes, ma'am. I'll be there when you say. Since you've got a thing for promptness." Jet got up with me and held out his arms.

I went into his embrace, trying not to melt into it, and gave him a stiff "strangers" hug.

I didn't know what else to say, so I left.

****

"I come bearing kittens! And coffee."

I opened the door to a beaming Jet who had a two pack of coffee and a brown bag. Buster struggled in his arms.

"Whatcha got there, mister? Besides two pounds of feline trouble?" The scent of cinnamon rolls wafted toward me.

"Two pounds of feline trouble and two delicious confections to fuel our cookie-baking efforts."

He ticked boxes I hadn't imagined I had on my checklist. Maybe I would wake up to a cold existence in an hour. It could be a dream.

Or a nightmare. I remembered Gail's dismissive words. *Second-hand Christmas sweater.* She'd been right about that.

"Right then. Put the cat…wherever. Just let him down. Coffee and pastries on the counter. I've got everything set up so we can get started."

"Sure." He handed me one of the coffees as he let Buster onto the floor. "This will be fun." He pointed to the mise en place with the coffee still in his hand. "Check you out. Y'all lined it up beforehand."

"That's what all good cooks do. Do you ever watch

23

any of the shows on TV?"

He followed me into the kitchen area. "I ain't much of a cook, but I've checked out a few. My dad has used some of the barbecue sauce one of them makes. Says it's good, but his is better."

"Sounds like a guy."

I waited for him to say something in rebuttal to that, but he took a sip of his coffee. "Let's get started so we can make it to the shelter in time."

We established a system. Once the ingredients were combined, I formed the balls of dough into the right shape and size, and then he rolled them in the sugar and set them on the baking sheets. When they had baked for about nine minutes—or until they were just brown—then we would press the unwrapped chocolate kisses on the cookies, enough so that the kiss stayed in the middle but the cookie didn't crack.

We made three dozen before Jet glanced at the time on the stove clock.

"We'd better let these cool down and pack them up for the road. We need to go soon."

I thought about not wearing the sweater again, but I'd said I would. It might be a while before the sting of Gail's words stopped haunting me. "Roger that. You put Buster away, and I'll transfer these to a paper plate so there's nothing to take back."

****

I wasn't sure what I expected from the shelter. Dozens of homeless milled around. Some were holding bags that Jet told me were pre-made meals. They were designed for those souls who could not face other people. He said just because they were on the outskirts didn't mean they lost their humanity. It was like this in all

24

cities. I'd never focused on it before.

But Jet had. He rescued kittens, homeless people…and solitary neighbors.

"What do we do at a soup kitchen?" Embarrassment burned my cheeks. What an ignorant, privileged question. I donated to charity with what little money I had, but I'd never thought to volunteer. Jet was legit too good to be true.

"Today it's about the chow line. During the holidays, lots of people help, so there will be a ton of folks there. All we have to do is give them meals. We'll see how you can be of service when we get there."

I was new to Portland, but I could have done this on my own. That failure pricked my conscience with points as sharp as Buster's claws. I didn't let those feelings show when we pulled up to the shelter and Jet parked before offering me his arm again as we headed toward the front door. A couple of people yelled his name as we approached. I watched as he greeted the person in charge with the air of the long-familiar. Then I was sent to help prepare the stuffing and slice the meats in the back kitchen.

Floyd, my partner, had a jovial air, but a hint of sadness marred his posture. He had an unkempt look for all that he was dressed in an oversized Christmas sweatshirt and a Santa hat. We made idle conversation as we worked in the buzz of activity. The shelter was decorated for the holiday, making it seem like it was just another community hall—if not for the people in front with ground-in dirt on their skin and haunted eyes.

"This is great," I said as I handed Floyd a platter of sliced ham.

"Yeah, it is," he agreed. "It's too bad it isn't like this

all year. February and March are as desperate for people but with much less support. It's easy to be charitable at Christmas."

I searched for words, but nothing suitable came to mind. Nothing I could say seemed appropriate. Jet was nowhere to be seen, but it didn't matter. This way of giving back, of helping others who weren't in a position to help themselves, was better than any party. Always before these people and their situations were abstract. Now I understood more how big the problem was. I felt great being part of the solution, if only for the day.

When the lines died down, Jet appeared, his Santa hat askew and his sweater dotted with bits of gravy and potatoes. The day was winding down, and the homeless were starting to thin out. Some were back out on the streets, and others were already in the scant rooms that the shelter had.

"We're done here. We can go anytime."

I looked at my companion for the day, who waved me off.

"You did good, Oriane. Thank you for your help. See you next year."

I nodded to him. "Or sooner. You never know."

He said nothing, telling me that dozens of people made that promise.

Jet had a pensive air when we drove back to the building. I let him take the lead and contented myself with enjoying the closeness of the small cabin. I shivered as the exertions of the day faded. Jet turned up the heat at my movement but didn't make any further comment.

He said little, and the tension grew with each passing mile. I reviewed the events of the day. I thought I'd done everything right, but I didn't know the protocol.

Maybe I'd offended someone, and he was too much of a gentleman to say it.

I started to get nervous. Sure, he had invited me, but that didn't give me claim to the rest of his day. It was mid-afternoon, and he could still go to other parties. I had no right to his time.

I found myself staring at his collar when we arrived at my door. Whatever I thought was developing between us was crumbling around me like ashes.

I'd known the man for a day, and having these sorts of fantasies about him was ridiculous. He collected strays, for heaven's sake.

I stuck my hand out, the awkwardness of the moment making me want to dash into my apartment. I was inadequate. Not that Jet made me feel that way. He was, if anything, too good, too sweet. This was a man who had tried to let Gail down the easy way until she forced his hand. He might be doing the same thing with me. Maybe he'd seen that I was interested and was backing away.

"Thanks for a nice twenty-four hours, Jet," I said, grateful that my voice was steady and impartial. I wished we had stayed strangers rather than feel I'd lost something intrinsic to my well-being.

He'd taken an unfamiliar person on a journey, and while it had been brief, it had still been kind of him. He didn't deserve my shattered expectations getting in the way of his generosity.

He stared at my hand and then shook it before releasing it. His palm was warm and dry, with calluses on the inside that suggested an active lifestyle. My skin tingled where he touched it, the brief contact a heady caress.

"You're welcome. Thanks for coming. The shelter is always a hell of an experience."

"It is. I learned a lot today." I didn't have words to say what I was feeling.

He seemed about to say something else, but then he stepped back. He cleared his throat and looked at my door. "I'll wait until you are safe. Merry Christmas, Oriane."

I wanted to kiss those delicious lips, but all I did was stare at my keys. "Thanks. Merry Christmas to you, Jet."

Then I opened the door and dashed inside. For a moment I heard nothing on the other side of the door, then he moved off, his steps retreating down the hall.

I'd blown it. I didn't know how, but I had.

I sighed and yanked off my sweater, which mocked me with its cheery colors and message of Christmas tidings. I didn't want to look at it now. Letting it fall into a heap on the floor, I went to change into my Christmas jammies.

****

The next morning I called my folks and got their rundown of the Christmas activities. Their cheer and sorrow at not having me there did a lot to soothe my wounded spirits. I was being ridiculous. I should take Jet's gift of his attention at the holiday for what it was—a kind gesture.

Next Christmas would be better. I'd have friends and established routines, and this time would be a memory. I could relay my exploits from the distance of time. I'd leave out Gail but would include the warm neighbor who had shown me other things to do on Christmas besides eat and open presents. I owed Jet for that. I would see him again. We lived two doors away, and at some point, we'd run into each other. But I wouldn't allow myself to let my fantasies override my good sense again.

Pancakes. That was the answer. Delicious, fluffy pancakes and some bacon. Bacon cured all ills.

Soon the smell of frying bacon permeated the apartment, mixing with the strong Christmas-blend coffee my folks had sent me with the pajamas. It would be all right. I had a lot to be grateful for and no business feeling sorry for myself.

I was preparing my plate when the familiar sound came through the door.

Meow, meow.

The plaintive cries were followed by the thump of a person's foot. The feet stopped in front of my door, and the meows cut off. I waited for other sounds, but none came. He was going to leave. He was going to take Buster, go back to his apartment, and not say hello. My spirits fell.

"Buster, what are you—ow!"

A thump echoed through the hallway, and then Jet muttered a curse, which was followed by a scrabble of kitten claws at the door. I could ignore it. That would be the smart thing to do.

I went to the door and opened it. Buster flew between my legs and into the apartment where he set upon grooming himself.

Jet gave me a sheepish smile. "Sorry. He smelled the bacon. I tried your trick, but he jumped over my foot and bolted."

He looked gorgeous and tousled—a man who had just risen from bed. He looked good enough to eat with my bacon.

29

"He's Houdini like that. Come on in. Buster already has."

Jet followed me inside, his gray sweatpants and Roll Tide T-shirt faded and well worn. I tried not to think what else he might have—or not have—on. My traitorous heart stuttered, despite all my lectures of the last twelve hours.

He nodded toward the red-and-green flannel on my body. "Nice jammies. I have a similar set at home."

I fluffed Buster's ruff, and he wriggled away from me, bounding into the living room. Soon he was intent on stalking a wild hair tie.

"It's a gift. We do it every year. Are you hungry? I can put more bacon on."

Jet grinned, and everything in me stood at attention.

"If you've got extra, I wouldn't mind some. That's right neighborly of you."

Yep. That was me. "Noted. I hear it's not good for cats." I waggled a finger at the fluff ball, who opened his mouth in a silent meow before chasing a dust mote that shone in the light coming in through the window. "No bacon for you, Buster."

"I was thinking of changing his name."

"You were? Why? Buster is a good name."

He shrugged. "I had to call him something. I was hoping for a T.S. Eliot 'three names of cats' inspiration, and one hit me."

T.S. Eliot. This guy. *Damn it*.

"I think it's called *The Naming of Cats*, but that doesn't matter. You are quoting poets, and that's fantastic."

"Yeah? It's not too nerdy?"

I should have better game than this, but everything

about Jet just tied me in knots. "Nerds will nerd. What were you thinking of changing it to?"

He gazed at the cat. "To Peanut. They're peanut blossoms, so it's because of the cookies. See, he's Peanut and…" Jet paused and looked ill at ease. "I thought maybe something was blossoming between us? I thought so, but after yesterday I wasn't sure."

My pulse stuttered, and I stared at him, open-mouthed. I took in his messy brown hair, the cute dimples that puckered when he smiled, and the uncertain air in his eyes. He held his hands out to me but let them drop when I didn't move.

"The way you said that is far nerdier than knowing Eliot. And a terrible pun." I blurted out the words in a rush, although they were not what I intended to say.

"My specialty." His uncertain expression shifted to wariness.

I opened my mouth, wanting to speak but not knowing what to say. It wasn't possible—it couldn't be. He could have a beautiful, together woman like Gail and not untidy me.

Peanut hovered by the counter, meowing toward the plate of cooling bacon. Jet groaned but then nodded. "Okay, maybe a little bit this once. Since it's still the holiday season."

I ruffled the little guy's fur before giving him a small piece, which he pounced on before carrying it off like a prize.

"You're keeping him?" He'd said he was considering it, but I didn't know if he'd made a decision. If he wasn't going to…I would.

"If nobody claims him, yeah. I can't imagine life without him."

"Yay. This kitten is something special."

He turned serious eyes back to me. "Oriane, about Christmas…what happened? We were having fun, then you were gone."

A million clever answers flowed through my mind, but the truth was best of all. "You were distant yesterday, and I wondered if I was misreading things."

"Distant?" He stared at me in disbelief for a moment, and then his expression cleared. "You mean after the shelter. I get that way sometimes. I wish I could do more, and seeing their misery reminds me of how lucky we are. That's what it was. Then you shoved me toward home, so I figured the night was over. I didn't realize how I acted. I sure am sorry."

I ducked my head to hide the heat that crawled up my cheeks. "I feel like a jerk. I thought you were done being nice and didn't need me around anymore. Even if all you were doing was playing with Buster…Peanut."

The cat in question darted into the living room to investigate an interesting dust mote again.

"You were gone before I could explain, and then I didn't know how to. Or even if you wanted me to. You weren't mad at me? You didn't want the day to end that soon?"

I thought of all the different ways to answer his question. His expression was beginning to shift again to hurt and pain. I had to fight past my fear and give this man the reply he deserved—the response that lay in my heart.

"Jet?" I touched his arm.

"Yeah?" He raked his hand through his hair and let it fall to his side. He started to turn away.

"I think Peanut is a fine name. I can't believe I'm

not alone thinking that something might be blossoming between us. I would like that."

He pivoted back to me, and the hurt that creased his cheeks and drew his lips down changed into a smile. "You're not putting me on?"

I was light-headed from emotion and relief, the knowledge that I hadn't been mistaking the signs making the future dance with incandescent possibilities.

Santa had brought me a present. The best one of all.

"I'm not. But Gail…" I flushed, angry with myself for even mentioning her name.

He made a dismissive gesture with his hand that attracted Peanut's attention. The kitten moved to pounce and then sat back and lay down, putting his head on his paws. I was distracted by the small feline until Jet closed the distance.

"I told you about Gail, and nothing has changed. To make it clearer, I told her again last night after you shooed me away that I hoped we could stay friends but that nothing would ever happen. She called when I got online. She was madder than a wet hen at my answer. She said she'd been 'friend-zoned' and not to call her for a while. I hate to hurt people, but it had to be done. Even if nothing happened with you, they weren't going to with her."

I blew out a breath. He'd turned Gail down without knowing that I was interested. He hadn't played the odds or weighed the options—he'd made a choice. I'd never met a guy like him before.

"Bet she didn't see that coming."

"Guess not. She was barking up the wrong tree. The final straw was how she treated you. I don't need people like that in my life."

"You are too good to be true."

His eyes were serious. "From the moment Peanut found his way to your door, I wanted to get to know you. You were terrific at the shelter, especially for your first time. You got me in a tizzy, and I guess it showed. It may have been one day, but that doesn't matter. There's something here, and I want to see where it goes. What do you say?"

I put my hands on his forearms and smiled up into his face. Relief had to be dancing on every corner of my expression. He gave me a shaky smile. It boggled my mind that I was his choice. It was a Christmas miracle.

"I'd like that."

He cupped my face in his hands and kissed me as though I were made of the finest china. It was delicate and sweet and all the more precious for its restraint. He buried his hands in my hair and then tucked my head against his chest, rocking me.

After a moment's hesitation, I tilted my face up and pressed my lips to his. He smelled of mint and tasted like home.

He slid his arms around me, embracing me the way I longed to be held. This was a full-body hug, all the right parts locked together. My body tingled where we touched, a slow-burning fire igniting under my skin.

When we separated, I was breathless.

"What are you doing for New Year's?"

I pretended to consider. "I was going to go join some wild party extravaganza downtown…nah. I had nothing going on. The perils of being in a new city."

He traced my cheek with his hand. "In that case, what about a night of watching the ball drop and drinking champagne? I'm going to do some volunteering on New

Year's Day, so I don't want to get hammered."

"That sounds perfect."

"To think I didn't know you existed a day ago. If not for that rascal of a cat, I wouldn't have knocked on your door."

I turned to look for the newly named Peanut, sure to find him bouncing around my living room, attacking invisible particles. When I found him, I pointed to him, sprawled out on the rug, his little belly rising and falling and his feet twitching in sleep.

"I think we've got ourselves a matchmaking kitten there."

He brushed the hair back from my eyes. "Yup. My favorite kind. He's a keeper. Now what about New Year's?"

"I'll get catnip if you'll get the champagne. I can't imagine anything more perfect."

When he kissed me again, a feeling of well-being washed over me. Everything had changed for me when Jet rescued Peanut. I just hadn't known it yet. Because of him I went from someone stranded at the holiday to a future full of possibilities. I looked forward to exploring every moment.

I met Peanut's gaze, who was blinking at us in contentment. He put his head on his paws and sighed.

My life was forever changed because of one mischievous, matchmaking kitten.

Red Velvet Crinkles and Christmas Sprinkles

by

Maria Imbalzano

Christmas Cookies Series

Dedication

To my warm, wonderful, and caring Dad who loved
Christmas. I miss you.

Chapter One

Why am I in my childhood bedroom? Isabella Simonetti scanned the very pink and extremely flowery room of her teens, her eyes heavy with sleep, her body still as a corpse. Until she heard the clatter of dishes and utensils from the kitchen, followed by the familiar voices of her parents.

She sprang up, and the warmth of the flower-explosion comforter fell away. *Oh no!* The scene in the managing partner's office came barreling back as if set on rewind and repeat at high volume.

"We're sorry, Bella, but I'm sure you understand." Peter Rose spoke for the entire law partnership. She was being fired.

The chill, then perspiring heat that had flooded her body at those words reappeared and threatened to overtake her. She inhaled a deep breath to ward off the nausea.

Throwing herself back on the bed, she pulled the frilly pastel comforter over her head, the throb of a new headache starting at the base of her skull. If she could only sleep for the next two months, wake up on January first with a new plan for the new year, and forget about the embarrassment that had become her life.

Three months had passed since she lost her job, three months that she worked with a headhunter to find a new one, and three months of "sorry, we're not hiring now, but we'll keep you in mind in the new year" from every law firm who even deigned to interview her.

"Bella, it's time for breakfast."

Her mom yelled up the stairs as if she were in high school.

"Be right there," she shouted, throwing the covers off, then sticking her feet into her favorite bunny slippers. *Jeesh*, she'd only been home since yesterday afternoon, and already she was reverting back to her childhood.

No need to dress. Her blue plaid flannel pajamas would serve her just fine. She was back home, in the place and amongst the people that wrapped her in warmth and love and comfort. And boy, did she need it.

Shuffling into the kitchen, she mumbled a "good morning" and went straight to the coffee maker for some much-needed caffeine.

"How'd you sleep?" asked her mom while she worked her magic at the stove, turning over sizzling bacon and flipping hot, buttered pancakes.

"Okay." No use complaining about the too-soft, too-short, too-narrow bed. Last night's restlessness had little to do with the fear of landing on the floor.

She sat in her seat at the table across from her dad, rolling her shoulders to get the kinks out. Within seconds a full plate of hot, fluffy pancakes and another of extra-crispy bacon—the exact way she liked it—appeared on the table.

"Mom, you didn't need to go to all this trouble. I usually have cereal or toast or a protein bar in the morning."

Her mother smiled. "Don't think you're getting this every morning. I'm much too busy at the shop. But I wanted to start your first day home off right. And since your dad is going to play golf, he could use a good breakfast as well."

Nothing, and certainly not carbohydrate-packed pancakes, would start this day off right, but she forked three onto her plate, drowned them in syrup, and grabbed two slices of bacon. The aroma alone could possibly inch her depression meter up from severe to tolerable. She dug in.

"Mmmmm," she hummed. "Mom, you do make the best pancakes. Thanks."

"You're welcome, honey. Do you have anything on your agenda for today? I was hoping you'd help at the shop."

"So there is a bribe associated with your welcome-home breakfast." Bella tried for a scoff, but the tiniest of grins broke through. Any time she came home for a few days, she ended up helping her mom and dad at Barb's Gift Cottage, a beautiful conglomeration of hand-crafted jewelry, silk scarves, books by local authors, decorative glassware, and specialty cookies. "Of course I'll help." *I have nothing else to do.*

"It's time to start decorating for Christmas. We always do that the first week of November, right after Halloween." Her mom's usual exuberance over this task appeared forced. Maybe she was tired.

Bella loved Christmas—at least in the past, when she wasn't dealing with her terrifying unemployment situation. Thus far, she hadn't shared with her parents the extent of her shame. Acknowledging that their Ivy-League-educated, scholarly daughter had been let go three whole months ago and couldn't find a replacement job was too humiliating. All she had revealed when she arrived was that she'd been unhappy working at a mega law firm and wanted to find something more suitable. As if she had voluntarily left the job yesterday.

To add insult to injury, she'd had to terminate her lease on her now-unaffordable, fabulous apartment on the Upper West Side. Which did happen yesterday. Her troubles were too soul crushing to blurt out upon arriving.

She ignored the little voice in her head encouraging her to come clean. Especially since she planned to live in her parents' house until she could find a job. Maybe she'd share at dinner tonight. After a bottle of wine.

The back door squeaked open, and a gust of air blew in before the door was firmly closed. "Good morning, Barb. Clive."

The guest entered and gave her mom a kiss on the cheek before slapping her dad on the back. Bella's mouth flew open as she watched the scene, a tiny gasp escaping.

Dean Jackson! What is he doing here?

"Honey, you remember Dean, don't you?" Her mom's smile grew much bigger than it had been all morning. "Your brother's friend from high school?"

"Of…of course I do." Bella fastened the top button of her pajamas before her hand flew up to assure her messy bun was still on top of her head. Fire flamed her face as she puzzled out the reason for his presence at seven thirty on a Wednesday morning. Or any time, for that matter.

"Dean's been like another son to us." Her dad beamed. "Ever since your brother took that job in Boston, he's helped us do whatever needs to be done around here or at the store. And he's my golf buddy."

Dean's gaze zeroed in on her, and her thoughts

fuzzed. She would have loved to slink upstairs, but no way was she going to get out of this chair, sporting flannel pajamas and bunny slippers. Was nothing sacred around here?

"It's going up to sixty-five degrees today." Dean rubbed his hands together. "Perfect for a round of golf."

Even though he was speaking to her dad, his gaze never moved from her face. Did she have syrup on her cheek or crumbs on her lips? She grabbed her napkin and brushed it over her mouth, getting both cheeks in its pass through.

She balled the napkin in her lap, but it didn't prevent her nails from digging into sweaty palms. Unfortunately, time had not diminished his gorgeousness—or the powerful hold he had on her traitorous libido. Confusion over colliding emotions stiffened her spine as her fluttering stomach made her queasy.

His deep voice cut into her agitation. "What brings you home, Bella? It's too early for Thanksgiving, and it's the middle of the week." He arched a brow over sparkling green eyes, mischievous eyes. "Did you get fired or something?" He chuckled at his joke.

"Of course she didn't." Her mom came to her rescue. "She decided Coley Green wasn't the right law firm for her. She's interviewing for other jobs."

Bella's throat closed, preventing her from speaking. But it didn't stop Dean from barreling into dangerous territory.

"How long are you visiting? A few days?"

All three of them looked toward her for an answer.

She cleared her throat. "I was thinking of staying until January. Unless I get hired to start somewhere right away." She hadn't planned to lie to her parents about this, but she couldn't air her embarrassing situation in front of Dean.

"That's wonderful, honey," said her mom. "We'd love to have you. You can work at the shop. One of our part-time sales people can't do it this year, and the holidays do get crazy. And you'll be here to prepare for Thanksgiving as well as Christmas." Her mother's smile radiated joy. "It will be nice to have our daughter here participating instead of only staying a day or two for each holiday before going back to work."

Fantastic. Her two month *vacation* to rest and rejuvenate had segued into an unpaid job as a sales clerk at her parents' gift shop. Would her flagging self-esteem survive this unintended demotion?

"Yes, that will be nice." Dean caught her eye, a question in his. As if he knew something wasn't right. "Well, Clive. Shall we get going? Our tee time is at eight thirty, and I want to hit a few balls before that."

Her dad stood, then gave her mom a kiss on her head. "I should be back around one to help you two with the Christmas decorations." He winked at Bella, as he often had when she was a child.

But instead of annoyance at reverting back fifteen years, a warm, fuzzy feeling enveloped her. "Have fun, Dad."

"What about me?"

Dean's teasing grin kicked at her heart, conjuring up the reason she hated him. Maybe hate was a strong word, especially after all this time, but intense dislike wasn't out of the question. "What about you?" Disdain, sprinkled with indifference, suffused her tone.

Thankfully, he let it go, but she caught the questioning look her mother threw her way.

As soon as her dad and Dean left, Bella rose and started clearing the breakfast plates. "That was awkward," she mumbled under her breath. She turned to her mom. "Does he always just walk in without knocking?"

"Yes, honey. It's Dean. He's been coming here since he and your brother were in high school."

"I know he and Scott were best friends back then, but they graduated thirteen years ago. Scott doesn't live here anymore. Why is Dean still hanging around?" Anger born from a long-ago wound reared up as if all those years hadn't intervened.

"He's been a great help to me and your dad. Once you and Scott chose to live elsewhere and Dean moved back from Florida, he's checked in on us. He lives in town, has a business here, and has become a good friend to your dad. They play golf together at least once a week until the weather gets bad."

"Why doesn't he hang out with people his own age?" The surliness in her voice wasn't drowned out by the running water as she scrubbed a pan with a vengeance. At least her mom couldn't see the scowl that accompanied her words.

"What's wrong, Bella? Don't you like Dean?"

She blew a loose tendril out of her face and rolled her eyes. "No. I don't like Dean."

"Why not? He's such a nice boy…man."

She dodged the specific reason. "Scott's friends were not nice to me in high school. Dean included."

"Why didn't you ever say anything, honey? I would have talked to them. Especially Dean. When his mother died, he looked to me to fill a little piece of that hole."

Her mom came over and rubbed her back, creating

a well of tears in Bella's eyes.

"He would have listened to me." A comforting arm wound over her shoulders, and her mom pulled her into a side hug. "He went through a rough time back then. Maybe his treatment of you was a result of the pain he was experiencing." She continued her comforting massage. "I know it's sometimes hard to let go of the past, but you were teenagers then. You've both grown and matured. You're a strong, independent, brilliant lawyer now—worlds past any lack of confidence you had as a teen. And Dean is a successful, creative business owner who would probably cringe if you told him now how he'd hurt you in the past."

Everything her mother said was true, but it didn't change the fact that all those feelings of inadequacy from years ago had swirled through her like a tornado the second he'd come through their back door.

Bella turned off the faucet and dried her hands, at a loss for words and close to tears. Her emotions ran high, stemming from her current situation and mixed with the angst over coming face-to-face with the boy, now man, who had ruined her hard-won confidence along with her romantic illusions thirteen years ago.

Her mom was right in certain rcspects. She was older, wiser, smarter, and stronger. But she would never forget what Dean had done to her.

And she wasn't about to let him forget it either.

Chapter Two

"What's with you and Bella?" Clive pulled his golf bag out of Dean's trunk and strapped it onto the back of the cart.

"What do you mean?" Dean figured he could play dumb, and Clive would let it go.

"She didn't seem all that happy to see you, and then when you teased her about whether she wanted you to have fun golfing, her retort was kind of caustic."

Ya think? She'd been downright rude. "I haven't seen her in a long time. Maybe she wasn't ready for a visitor so early this morning." That seemed plausible. Because he'd rather that than what could possibly be the real reason. But would she be carrying around a grudge for all these years? Doubtful. She'd left this town in the dust the minute she left for college.

He exhaled. She'd looked pretty sexy, in an adorable sort of way—with those flannel pj's and her hair falling out of her ponytail—or whatever it was. Just the right amount of rumpled. If she was his girlfriend, he would have had her back in bed in seconds.

But she wasn't.

And from the reception he'd received this morning, that possibility would never come close to fruition.

Dean pursued a different vein to the same topic. "You seemed surprised that she was staying until January. What's the story?"

Clive raised a brow. "I'm not sure. When she showed up yesterday, she said she left her job at Coley Green because it wasn't the right place for her. It's a huge firm, and she works with multi-million-dollar companies, but she's behind the scenes. Doing research, writing memos or proposals or whatever it is she does."

"I guess she has to put in the time before she graduates to working directly with clients—at least at those big law firms. Maybe she'd be better off at a smaller firm. Has she ever considered working here in Princeton?" Then maybe he could crack that icy façade and make her melt in his arms.

Clive laughed. "Not Bella. She's always been all about the big city. She loves New York—the millions of people, the electricity she likes to call it. I don't know. I never felt comfortable there. Too big. Too noisy. But she's loved it since she went on buying trips with Barbara for the shop."

Dean set up his tee on the first hole, but his mind was whirring. "Is she seeing anyone?"

Clive shrugged. "Not that I know of. Not anyone she's ever mentioned to Barb or me. I guess if she was, he wasn't that important. I'm not sure she's had time to date. She worked sixty to seventy hours a week." He paused and pointed his driver at Dean's tee. "Are you going to hit or what?"

Dean put his head down and stood over his ball, taking a practice stroke before whacking it right into the trees on the right. *Great.* If this was any indication of how he was going to play today, he should give up right now.

"Nice shot." Clive smiled as he set up his tee. "You'd better get your mind off Bella and onto the game, or I'm going to clean your clock."

He was right. No use wondering what her attitude stemmed from this morning. Better to have a conversation with her—alone.

Once he put his mind to it, the rest of the game went much more smoothly, and the fresh air, warm sun, and challenge of the match all did what they were supposed to do—free his brain from work and any other problem weighing him down.

When they finished, they headed back to the car with the golf cart to stow their clubs.

"How's business?" Clive asked, not an unfamiliar question. The two of them often talked about the ups and downs of owning a small business in town.

"Good. My piece of it slows down a little in the winter, but some people still like to hire me now to create their landscape plans for the spring. When I'm not in my office or working with clients, I go over and help my brother with the nursery. Christmas trees will be there in a few weeks, along with the wreaths and poinsettias. You know how insane it gets."

"That I do." Clive paused as if pondering the season about to befall them.

"How's your shop doing? I haven't been called in to help move any cases and tables around lately."

Clive exhaled a troubled breath. "To tell you the truth, I'm not sure we're going to make it much longer."

"What? Yours is the most perfect gift shop I've ever been in."

"It is beautiful, thanks to Barb. But the foot traffic is getting less and less. It's too easy for people to go online and get what they want."

"Sure, but then they can't see or touch the

merchandise or meet the local authors. Or smell Barb's fresh-baked cookies. In my opinion, that's the best thing about your shop."

"I hear you, Dean. And of course, I'd like nothing better than to say things are going well. We're hoping the Christmas season will make up for lost revenues over the summer and fall, but it will actually take a miracle to finish in the black this year."

"Are you thinking of closing after the holidays?" Dean couldn't imagine not having Barb's Gift Cottage in town. While he wasn't one for buying many of their crafty wares, he made up for it in cookie purchases. Anytime he needed something to bring to a dinner party or to send as a thank-you to a client, he headed to their shop for his favorite dessert—red velvet crinkles.

"We are thinking about it." Clive's eyes clouded. "Barb is in denial. You know how much of herself she puts into that shop. She adores it—especially because she's able to support the local crafts people and authors. And she loves making those cookies."

Not only did Barb thrive as the social proprietor of the shop—greeting every customer and helping them find that perfect gift—but Clive's life revolved around their business as well. He was the financial guru and inventory organizer. He kept the books, paid the taxes, hired help when necessary, inventoried the shelves, and moved display cases and tables at Barb's request, making her image of the store come to life. She was the heart. He was the backbone. And together they made it all seem easy.

"Does Bella know?"

"No. Not yet." Clive grimaced as if it would be a painful conversation.

And of course, it would be. Although Bella hadn't come back home after college to get involved in her parents' business, she had always worked there on weekends and holidays in high school and vacations from college. Whenever he and Scott were called upon to help move a display, Bella was there "fixing" things to her liking.

That was the one place where he could interact with her without judgment, since he was helping her parents. By eleventh grade she had morphed into a beauty, and he'd had a hard time keeping his gaze from seeking her out. One day he recalled her standing by the jewelry display, her long, dark hair pulled to one side of her neck while she held up colorful gemstones to her ear. He snuck up behind her and whispered, "Those look great on you," or something equally lame. Her face flamed red, but their gazes locked in the mirror for what seemed like minutes.

She had smelled like vanilla and cinnamon, and her skin looked so soft, so silky. How he'd wanted to kiss her vulnerable neck.

But Bella was off-limits.

That didn't preclude some fairly steamy dreams about her, though. In order to keep her in the bubble where she belonged, he teased her the same as her brother did, to assure that nothing came of his illicit flirtations.

Now was a different story. Bella would be around for at least two months, maybe longer. What would be the harm in getting to know the forbidden girl—now woman—who had starred in some pretty heavy fantasies?

Chapter Three

Bella unzipped her suitcase and placed a few blouses and sweaters neatly on her bed. Opening her closet door to collect some hangers, she stopped short. Her prom gown—a fuchsia, silk sheath with spaghetti straps—still hung toward the back, covered in plastic. The punch to her gut was almost physical.

Deep feelings of defeat, disappointment, and hurt crowded her already reeling brain. *I'm really sorry, Bella, but I have to cancel. Something's come up.* That was the only explanation she'd received from Dean for dashing her dreams and reigniting her insecurities.

She exhaled, blowing away the bad memories that swirled before her in a nostalgic haze. Pushing herself to unpack the rest of her clothes, she tossed them in drawers with no thought for order and called forth her inner counselor to banish the past. After all, that sad chapter in her life had taken place thirteen years ago. She was a different woman now—strong, independent, and brilliant according to her mother. She'd best wrap those qualities around her as armor and forget her and Dean's ancient history.

Eventually, she pulled herself together enough to meet her parents at the shop at one, as promised. The designer jeans and cashmere sweater she donned, although part of her wardrobe, had never been worn until today. She lived in conservative suits while at the office and yoga pants and tees when in her apartment.

The unusually warm weather for November encouraged her to walk to the shop, a mile and a half from her parents' house. The fresh air and exercise would do her good. Maybe she could rid herself of all negative thoughts for the time being and focus solely on the holidays to come while working side by side with her parents. The past was a distant memory, and her future had yet to be written. She would not dwell on the mess her life was in right now. She'd given herself two months off to get away from it all. And that's exactly what she planned to do.

Besides, what kind of life had she been leading? The three years of law school were nonstop study— Saturdays and Sundays included—and the job she'd aimed for and secured had basically the same schedule. Although she did take off most Sundays—unless facing a deadline.

Poring over merger contracts, bank loan details, corporate documents, and financial records, all in her day's work in representing shareholders or partners in business deals, was not exactly what she'd thought she'd be doing after three years at the firm. Her job of analyzing, then summarizing the salient information and putting it into legal memoranda form for whatever senior lawyer she was working with was getting tedious. Unfortunately, the fifth and sixth year associates were still doing the same thing.

Maybe she shouldn't look at the circumstances that brought her to this point as a disaster. Perhaps they were the kick she needed to leave the job she disliked, since she would never have left otherwise. The money alone was enough to keep her handcuffed to the firm for life, but the prestige of working at one of the premier firms in Manhattan was the real shackle. At least now she could think about what career move would make her happy.

All her life she'd wanted to appear successful—enough to make her be seen by her peers. In high school, she strived to be the best academically because she was never going to be popular socially. Her lack of gymnastic skills precluded her from being a cheerleader, her tone-deaf ear kept her out of the marching band, and her timidity had her running in the opposite direction when auditions were scheduled for the school play. So she stuck her nose in her books and vowed to be the smartest if she couldn't be part of the "in" crowd.

Scott and Dean were, of course, major members of that group. Football players had VIP cards. However, Bella could move around their edges, soaking in their aura. Especially when Scott invited his friends over to their house. She'd studied the "it" girls with a discerning eye—what they wore, how they talked, how they acted. By junior year she had shed her glasses for contacts, started watching what she ate, and exercised by taking ballet classes. She'd let her medium-length hair grow long, got rid of the bangs, and replaced her baggy jeans with more flattering ones.

All to no avail. Scott and his friends, including Dean, continued to tease her as if she were still that awkward, gawky ten-year-old with braces and overalls.

Unless Dean happened to be in the same vicinity as Bella in the store—without Scott attached to his hip. On those occasions he would catch her eye and smile or say something that would make her skin tingle.

Those butterfly-inducing moments had caused her to make the biggest mistake of her life. The reason why she still harbored animosity toward the "wonderful guy" her parents couldn't live without.

Arriving at Barb's Gift Cottage much too soon, she inhaled a cleansing breath before entering the shop.

"Hi, Mom. I'm ready to decorate." She looked around at the beautiful displays set out so lovingly by her mother—variations on a hue were grouped together but looked like a rainbow when seen as a whole. "Are you sure you want to ruin your artistry with Christmas decorations? If I was in here looking for a gift, I'd want one of everything." She fingered an aqua and ginger silk scarf before picking up the turquoise, dangly earrings that were paired with it.

"Thanks, Bella. You know how I love to play around exhibiting our merchandise. But I'm excited to move into the holiday season. The Christmas ornaments and nutcrackers make the store look so festive."

Bella scanned the shop. "No customers? I know it's Wednesday afternoon, but there's usually a few people milling about every time I come in."

"Oh, you know how it is." Her mother dismissed her words with a wave of her hand. "It will give us time to go back into the storeroom and pull out the boxes we'll need. Let's go."

Bella shrugged out of her jacket and hung it on a hook in the hall leading to the storage area. She followed her mom, took direction of which boxes to take out, and got to the heavy-lifting part of the job. "Shouldn't we wait for Dad to get back from golf? These boxes are heavy." She struggled down the hallway and into the store before dropping it near the cash register.

"They'll be here soon."

"They?" It couldn't be.

"Yes. Your father and Dean. Dean promised to help."

Great. "Doesn't he have a job to get back to?"

"He's a landscape architect. Although he starts getting busy again right after the new year, he slows down in November and December."

"Humph," was all she could say. She eyed the cookie case. "Why aren't there any cookies?" She was dying for a sugar cookie with sprinkles.

"We sold out by noon today. I make only enough so there are fresh cookies every day."

"How many do you make?"

Her mom headed back to the storeroom, mumbling her answer, but Bella didn't catch it.

Just then the bell over the door signaled a customer. Bella glanced up to see if their guest was here to browse or needed help, but no customer materialized. It was her dad with Dean in tow.

She had to admit he was even more striking than in high school. His light brown hair, sweeping from left to right in a perfect wave of silk, still had sun streaks from the summer, no doubt enhanced while playing on the links. And those green eyes had always been like flashing gemstones that sucked her in. But the best was his roguish smile—half teasing, half serious, but permanently heart-stopping.

Her best bet would be to prevent any cause for cheerfulness. Yet his intense frown was also mesmerizing. Staying away from him altogether seemed the ideal solution, but her parents had different ideas. Of course, her surliness toward him might make him rethink his charitable desire to help.

"Hi, Bella. How's it going?" Even that simple

greeting came with a full-blown smile.

She was screwed. "Fine." She got right to the point—no friendly chitchat. "If you and Dad bring the boxes up front from the storeroom, Mom and I will take care of the decorating. You won't have to stay."

"Are you kidding? I love to decorate for Christmas. I've been helping your parents do it for the past few years while you've been AWOL."

She blew an errant strand of hair out of her eye. "I wasn't AWOL. I was working. In New York. I couldn't up and leave on a Wednesday afternoon to come home and decorate."

There came that half-teasing, half-serious smile. To avoid it, she started pulling Christmas balls hung on red-and-green silk ribbons from the large box she'd brought out.

"I can help you hang those in the window. I hid the hooks above the molding last year so we don't have to remove them every year."

"Clever." Her sarcastic tone couldn't be mistaken.

"We'll need a ladder," he determined. "I'll get it from the back, then you can hand me the balls, and I'll attach them."

She slitted her eyes at him. "I want to hang the balls. You can do something else."

"Fine. But it takes two for this job. You don't want to be going up and down the ladder each time you hang a ball. It's inefficient."

He had a point. She'd have to bury her reluctance to work with him at the risk of coming up with some other childish excuse.

Once Dean brought the ladder to the window, she climbed up three steps and took the first ball from him.

Not a well-thought-out plan since her butt was now at his eye level.

"Can you stand over here, please?" She pointed to the other side of the ladder.

"It's better if I stand behind you, to spot you. In case you lose your balance." His grin emerged, and she gritted her teeth to prevent a growl.

Inhaling, she reached up to tie the ribbon on the hook. Her sweater inched over her midriff, giving him a view of her torso. This day just couldn't get any worse. If she hadn't been so stubborn in demanding that she hang the ornaments, she'd have the pleasure of staring at his physique, not the other way around.

She aimed to accomplish this job in record time so she could move on to the next task—something solitary and away from the man who scrambled her brain. Each time he handed her a ribbon, his fingers grazed hers, as if on purpose, and warm tingles shot up her arm. When she deigned to take a glimpse into his eyes, they held hers—as if his captive—for a moment too long, scattering all thought. When she reached over a little too far, so as not to have to move the ladder again, his warm hands encircled her bared waist, causing a riot in her core.

"Can't have you falling," he said, his voice raspy. Sexy.

She closed her eyes for a moment. "You can let go now. We're done here."

Instead of releasing her, he guided her down the steps. Although her back was to him, his familiar scent— leather and sandalwood—had her reeling. How could this fragrance from so long ago affect her like this?

Refusing to turn and look at him, she pulled away,

tugging at her sweater. "Thanks. I'll put the snowflakes on the windows. You can help my dad with the lights."

She started to walk away, but he grabbed her arm and spun her around.

"What's going on, Bella? It's like you don't want to be near me. Did I offend you in some way?"

As the blood rushed from her head, she took an unsteady breath. She could feel his eyes study her, but she couldn't look at him, afraid a stray, uncalled-for tear would slip out.

"We'd better get back to work." She extricated her hands from his, and a chill immediately took over. "I'll go get the window decals."

Disappointment cast a shadow over his eyes. "Okay, then." He exhaled. "I guess I'll help your dad with the lights."

She turned, berating herself for not stating her problem with him. Keeping things bottled up was not good for her mental health, and she'd not only missed her opportunity to confront Dean head on with her gripe against him, but she'd been tiptoeing around the truth of her current predicament with her parents.

Since when had she lost her courage, her moxie, her grit?

She must have left it all in the managing partner's office when she was fired.

The time had come to get it back.

Chapter Four

Arriving in the kitchen the next morning, Bella was prepared. She'd showered, dressed, and put on some mascara in case they had a visitor. But only her mom and dad sat at the table eating toast, drinking coffee, and embarking on what appeared to be a very serious conversation.

"What, no Belgian waffles this morning?" She made her own coffee and toast before joining them.

"I told you yesterday, honey, that was a welcome-home breakfast. No more of those until Christmas morning. I have to get to the shop and bake cookies." Within minutes, her mom got up and put her dishes in the dishwasher.

Bella looked at the clock. Eight fifteen. The shop usually opened at ten, giving her mother an hour and a half to fill the bakery case. "I'll come with you. I can help you bake." Best to keep her mind off her dilemma, despite her questionable expertise in the kitchen.

"Sure. Let's go. We'll see you there, Clive."

As they got in the car, Bella noticed her mother's furrowed brow. "Is everything okay? Doesn't Dad usually go to the shop with you?"

"He does. But he has some errands to do this morning. The bank, the post office. He'll be there by the time we open."

"What cookies are you making today?"

"Since we decorated the store for Christmas, I want to make gingerbread cookies. They're such a hit around the holidays."

"Only one kind? I know the cookie case isn't big, but don't you make a variety?"

"On weekends I do. But Thursdays don't warrant it."

They got to work right away, with her mother directing her to pull out all the ingredients—flour, sugar, eggs, cinnamon, ground ginger, light molasses, baking soda, and butter—as her mom preheated the ovens, greased the trays, and accumulated the utensils they'd need, including Christmas-themed cookie cutters.

"What other cookies do you make during the holidays?"

"Red velvet crinkles, butter balls, biscotti, cannoli cookies, snickerdoodles. Whatever I'm in the mood to make."

Her mom never used a recipe, knowing her craft by heart, but Bella could use written instructions.

"You should write your recipes down so I could cover for you some mornings. Then you wouldn't have to come in early."

"I'm used to it, and I really enjoy the feeling of satisfaction I get while baking. It's also a good time to try out new recipes."

Bella let her offer go with a shrug. She didn't actually want to do it anyway. Her mom did most of the work, stating it was easier for her to do it herself than direct her daughter, especially since Bella was a little casual in measuring ingredients. Even so, she enjoyed being in the shop's kitchen, with memories of her younger days sitting on the stool watching her mom like this settling around her like an angora blanket.

They made—or more accurately, her mom made—four dozen cookies and filled the small case right before ten.

"Just in time." Bella looked at the clock on the opposite wall, stole a snowman-shaped cookie, still warm from the oven, then went to unlock the front door. "This place looks magical, Mom. I love the nutcrackers you've placed around the store—color coded to match the merchandise. And the decorations on the Christmas tree are so creative."

Her mom had used earrings, necklaces, and scarves instead of glass balls and garland.

"You have such a flair for enticing displays."

"It's what I love to do." An uncharacteristic melancholy tinged her voice.

The bell over the entrance tinkled, and a customer came in to buy a dozen cookies. Ten minutes later another customer arrived and purchased six cookies. Bella straightened some of the crafts on the central tables, not because they needed fixing, but for something to do. Her dad arrived around noon but went straight back to the office to work on whatever he did behind the scenes.

Another two hours passed, and no one came to the shop. "Is it usually this slow during the week?"

"Unfortunately, yes. We started closing on Tuesdays in addition to Mondays, since it didn't seem worth it to spend the money on electricity. But once we hit the week before Thanksgiving, we'll be open seven days a week through New Year's Eve. Except for Christmas Day of course. We're hoping business will pick up."

Her dad came into the store, rubbing his forehead as if to ward off a headache. "Any sales?"

"A few cookies. How'd it go at the bank?" asked her mother. "You didn't say anything when you came in."

Her dad looked at Bella, then back at her mother, as if pointing out that their child was in the room.

Her mother answered the unstated question. "We should let Bella in on what's going on. Maybe she'll have an idea."

She looked to her dad, confused. "Is there something I could help with?"

"I went to our bank this morning to see about another small business loan, but they're not inclined to give it based on our declining sales."

Whoa. This couldn't be good, especially since her dad said this would have been an additional business loan. "How much do you need?" Not that she had any spare funds after flying through her meager savings while living in Manhattan without a job.

"We wanted seventy thousand but would take less."

"That's a lot of money." The dire news punched her in the gut. "What do you need it for?" Perhaps they were only looking for a cushion.

He ran his hands through his thinning grayish hair. "We're behind on our property taxes, which as you know, are astronomical in Princeton. And we're more than ninety days late in paying some of our vendors. They won't send us any more merchandise until we're paid up."

Her mom chimed in. "It's not like we're selling their merchandise anyway. I've had the same scarves, wallets, and jewelry on that table on the left for the past nine months. I don't understand. They're beautifully crafted, made of high-quality materials, and reasonably priced."

"You need customers to come into the shop in order to sell, Barbara."

Bella had never heard a harsh word between her parents, and although her dad was not angry with her mom, she could feel the tension in the air.

She stepped in, putting on her corporate lawyer hat to discuss and hopefully work through their problems. "Your foot traffic has died down. Is that the main problem, or is there more to it?"

"That's the problem." Her mom looked pained. "When you were growing up, we thrived. People were constantly visiting Princeton, whether parents of the students at the university or those who just wanted to walk around a quaint town and shop. We also had the locals who needed gifts for house parties or birthdays or other major milestones. This was the place to go. But in the past few years, we've seen fewer and fewer customers." She heaved a sigh. "We don't know what to do."

"How is your website doing? Are you tracking clicks?"

"Website." Her father nearly barked. "We don't have a website."

Although she hadn't been tuned in to her parents' business for years, how was that possible? "Mom, Dad, you need a website. A place where people could go to see what you're selling. That's how shoppers do it these days. You must know that from purchases you've made online."

Her mother frowned. "Well, yes. I go to Amazon like everyone else. They don't have a store, so it's the only way to purchase anything from them."

Bella took a breath. Being annoyed wouldn't help. She needed to get them up to speed—if it wasn't already too late.

She looked around the store. "You said people aren't coming in much to shop for gifts, but they are coming in for cookies, right?"

Her mom nodded.

"What if you streamlined and expanded on what you do sell? And market that."

"You mean only sell cookies?" Her father's tone, highlighted by his scrunched forehead, couldn't be more negative.

"Your business plan clearly isn't working anymore. We need to focus on a website and possibly sell your crafts there." The shocked looks on their faces made her double back—a little. "Okay. You can sell some of your wares here. But make the best use of your space for what you do sell. Cookies. You only have one tiny case for baked goods right now. Maybe add coffee, tea, hot chocolate. And capitalize on your amazing baking skills. That's what brings your foot traffic in. People want home-baked goods fresh out of the oven. The other stuff they could get on Etsy."

"Etsy?"

Her mom's perplexed scowl made her laugh. A true neophyte when it came to internet shopping.

"It's a global internet marketing site where people sell things they make. Personalized gifts, handmade jewelry, invitations, crocheted and knitted items. You name it, it's probably available for purchase. And there's no overhead, so the cost is less than what you'd sell it for here."

"But people like to see the things they're buying,

touch them. Decide if the quality is up to par. They can't do that by looking at photos on a computer."

"That's true. But they could return it if they don't like it. Unless it's personalized. The problem these days is that people don't have enough time to shop. They go online during their lunch hour or while they're watching TV at night or when they can't sleep and root around for what they're looking for. It's easy. I do it when I need a gift."

Her mom huffed. "If you came home once in a while, you'd be able to buy some very nice, high-quality gifts here."

Bella bit her tongue. "You're right. But my job required me to be in the office ten hours a day." A punch to her gut emphasized the reality that she no longer had a job. "Do you have a pad of paper? I'll work on a plan for you to consider."

At least she could make herself useful doing that since she had no customers to help.

For the rest of the day, she worked on a diagram rearranging cases, moving tables, eliminating many of the soft goods they sold—at least for now. Instead of one miniature cookie case, she requisitioned the jewelry display cases and lined them up on her drawing along the right hand side of the store, closest to the kitchen. She moved the bookcases over to the wall behind the display cases to use as backup for more cookies or cute decorations that would enhance the area. This would take up half the store. If they cleared off some of the tables with scarves, capes, wallets, and other accessories, they could use those for people to sit and enjoy their cookies with a hot beverage. She drew in three tables toward the back left side of the store to sell whatever gifts were the most popular. During this season it would be hand-crafted Christmas decorations and knitted scarves, hats, and gloves. The rest of their inventory they'd store for the time being—or sell through their currently nonexistent website.

With pad and pencil in hand, she sat on the stool at the cash register and began the major work of writing up a business plan. She started with what needed to be done first—rearranging the entire store to conform to her diagram—then segued into designing a website and assorted marketing ideas for consideration, including changing the name of the shop. She smirked. As if that would happen.

When she looked out the window, darkness shrouded the street.

She stood and stretched, scanning the overstocked store. Her mom was helping a customer—a good sign—with some ornaments and holiday decorations. She looked at the clock, almost six thirty.

Her stomach rumbled. Thankfully, the store closed at seven tonight, and she could go home to eat something. And share her great ideas with her parents.

Although she knew, deep down, it would take a Christmas miracle to get them on board.

Chapter Five

"In my opinion, you're moving too fast." Dean sat across the table from Bella as she presented her ideas to her parents.

She narrowed her eyes at him. "I wasn't aware that you had a say in this matter."

Just because her dad had telephoned Dean the second they had finished dinner to invite him over for this discussion didn't mean he had veto power. And just because he made her blood sizzle when he'd wrapped his warm hands around her waist didn't give him an advantage in her eyes.

Her dad intervened. "Honey, we trust Dean. He's been our sounding board for the last few years, and he knows the Princeton community. He also knows a thing or two about running a small business."

"Well, I know a thing or two as well. I'm involved in representing dozens of clients who own businesses, and I am very aware that you can't sit back and hope that people show up. You have to have a business plan. And a marketing plan. It doesn't appear that you have either."

Her mom patted her hand. "Your clients have businesses that are much bigger than ours. I'm sure your advice to them is excellent. But this is a small town, not a big city."

At her firm in New York, she'd been valued—her ideas considered. She'd been seen and heard as a worthy colleague and counselor by the attorneys she worked for. Here, at home, she was being patronized. She dug deep to keep the emotion out of this discussion as she had done when sharing her ideas with the partner in charge of a specific client. Although this was different. She was facing her parents, whom she loved and wanted to help. But she couldn't if they continued to put up barriers to every idea she had.

And Dean was of no assistance. She'd expected him to jump on her bandwagon, and instead he was being as conservative and pigheaded as they were. She wanted to scream. But that wasn't the way to win them over.

She stood and paced the kitchen, counting to ten to bring calm within. "I know change is hard. And I know you've both worked your whole lives in that store to make it successful. And it was. But you're telling me it's not now. That you need money to pay the taxes and your vendors, and you can't get a loan. To me, that's major trouble. Which means you won't have a business for much longer."

She looked at each one of them with her practiced counselor gaze in her effort to convey her knowledge, experience, and wise advice.

Dean spoke first. "Your idea is to completely change the shop within days, to go from a unique space for gifts to a bakery." He shook his head. "It's an entirely different business."

Her parents murmured words of agreement.

She swallowed her annoyance. Was anyone listening? They would have no business at all if they kept to the same script.

"I know it's a huge adjustment. But it's not completely different. Mom, you sell cookies now. And you said that's what people are coming in for. That's amazing, given that you have room enough for only six-dozen cookies. Everyone has always loved your baked goods. You have so many fabulous recipes. Christmas cookies are something everyone wants. And they apparently don't want silk scarves and hand-crafted necklaces."

"Let's say we do more cookies around Christmas." Her mom allowed at least the thought to permeate. "What happens in January? We're back to square one."

"No. Every month you do cookies to celebrate the holiday. January could be the new year and…winter wonder." She'd have to work on that one. "Valentine's Day is in February, but the whole month you could celebrate love. March would commemorate spring and April, Easter. We go through the year and make each month a holiday for cookies." She glanced at her mom to see if a hint of excitement sparked over her plan. "And don't forget, you'd still have a few tables with gifts that would go along with the holiday."

She hoped that not getting rid of the gifts altogether would soften her mom's hesitance over the whole idea.

Her mom glanced over at her dad. "Clive, what do you think?"

"I agree with Dean. Barb's Gift Cottage has been in Princeton for thirty years. You don't decide one day to revamp the entire business. Get rid of the old, make way for the new. It doesn't make any sense to me."

Bella bit her tongue before responding, reminding herself to stay cool. "Okay. I'm open to anything. Let's talk about your ideas to stay afloat." She sat, poised with her pad in front of her, pen in hand.

Silence.

She looked directly at her dad first, eyebrow arched. "I'm listening." Then she scanned over to Dean.

Her gaze moved up to his eyes—sea green in the harsh kitchen light but beautiful just the same.

His gaze locked with hers and held her hostage—an unwilling prisoner to his warden. All ire morphed into a swirling eddy of primal lust, and she felt herself disappearing into his aura. She needed to save herself as well as her ego. Fighting the pull, she surfaced, blinking to clear her eyes, inhaling to bring her back to the present.

She disconnected and glanced at her parents. Had they noticed she'd been missing?

The smallest smile quirked Dean's lips—surely acknowledging her lapse into Dean-land. She reached for the annoyance she'd let slip from her grasp and pulled it back into her arsenal.

"I haven't heard your brilliant ideas yet." Her voice was brittle, cold.

Nothing.

Her mom jumped in, presumably to get the two men off the hook, although they didn't deserve saving. "The Christmas season does better than the rest of the year." Her tone was thin, limp.

Bella's sigh echoed around the room. "I can't help you succeed if you're not willing to try something different." She shook her head. "Fine. You'll get through the Christmas holidays. Hopefully, you'll make enough to pay the real estate taxes and your overdue vendors. Then, come January, you'll start over with the same problems. Is that the plan?"

Her stomach knotted, and her body ached with the stress of taking on her parents' burden. But she couldn't make them convert. All she could do was impart her wise counsel.

"Why don't we sleep on it tonight?" suggested her mom. "It's such a drastic change that we're having a hard time digesting it."

"Good idea," agreed Bella. "I'm exhausted. I'm going to bed." She rose, the weight of their problems pressing down on her.

Her clients at the law firm benefited from the advice she outlined in memos to the partners after having worked through the issues behind the scenes. Of course, they were paying for that advice and looking for solutions. And they were hearing it from the more-experienced lawyers who were the ones who met with the clients. Perhaps her parents didn't trust her. She'd only been out of law school for a few years. They didn't know how much she'd learned about small businesses through her day-to-day work.

But if they decided on no change, she'd have to let it go. And they'd sink or swim on their own terms.

She'd be back in the city in January, dealing with her own sinking ship.

Chapter Six

With eight hours of sleep behind her, she thought she'd feel better, but her body ached, and her eyelids remained at half-mast. Coffee might help, but since she never knew if Dean would be sitting in the kitchen—or just showing up—she headed for the shower.

The hall bathroom at her parents' house was huge by Manhattan standards, with a double-stall shower and a much more forceful stream than in her apartment in the city. She blew out a breath. Her former apartment. How had she gone from one of the firm's brightest associates to an out-of-work, homeless woman?

She felt worse than she had in months. Not only was her life upside down, but her parents would soon be joining her. They needed to act while that was still possible. The burden was on her to convince them to turn this around so their lives wouldn't be upended at their age. Not that they were old—mid-fifties—but having to reinvent themselves at this stage could prove problematic.

At least she had time on her side.

She stood under the steaming hot water, hoping it would inject some life and spirit into her, for she would need it. She moved by rote through her routine until she was ready to face her parents' ultimate decision.

Half dreading the discussion to come, she tiptoed down the stairs and into the kitchen. Her mom and dad sat at their usual spots, a pad of paper before her mom.

"Good morning, Bella. I hope you slept well."

Her mom had to be kidding. She arched a brow as her response.

"We have a lot of work to do today. We've decided to try your plan."

Bella stopped midway to the coffee maker and turned. "You did?"

Her father responded. "We realized we have no other choice. You were right. We'll be facing the same problems in January unless we do something to stop the bleeding."

"So," her mother said, "we're going to box up all the novelties that aren't Christmas or holiday themed, rearrange the store as you have it on your diagram, and start selling cookies." A heavy sigh escaped. "I'm hoping that when one door closes, another one opens."

Bella swallowed, elation and fear colliding in her brain. "That's great," she squeaked.

Her father stood and brought his coffee mug to the sink. "I already called Dean."

Of course you did.

"He'll gather some of the guys that work at the nursery to come over and help with the cases and tables once we've cleared almost everything out."

"Wonderful." Bella gulped her coffee. She needed it to jolt her into action. "I'll help the two of you organize and pack up what's going into storage after I take photos of everything for the website. Then I'll start on the marketing side of it. Mom, I'll need your list of holiday cookies."

"I put it together earlier." She ripped off the top page from her pad, which enumerated at least twenty types, many starting with the word *Italian*.

"Mom, you're going to have to get rid of the cultural description. Italian lemon cookies should merely be lemon cookies."

"Why? These recipes have been handed down from your great-grandmother. You love them. Everyone loves them."

"True. But this is a business. You are not selling Italian cookies. You're selling holiday cookies. To everyone. Whether they're Jewish, Polish, German, Argentinian, Egyptian, Arab, whatever. You should probably look online for the most popular holiday cookies in America."

The disappointment on her mother's face advised her to take a softer approach. "I'm not saying you shouldn't make your cannoli cookies or biscotti or pizzelles. I'm suggesting that you diversify." She went over to her mother and draped her arm over her shoulders. "This is a big step, and I know it's hard. I'll try to be less of your business planner and more of your daughter."

Her mother's voice caught. "I'd like that."

For the next five hours, she took photos on her phone and helped her parents pack up books, silk scarves, jewelry, hand-painted glasses, ceramics, and miscellaneous gift items. If the cookie idea worked, she'd help her mom sell these beautiful items on their website or at craft shows around the state at a later date. They worked in silence, as if at a funeral, and Bella experienced firsthand the weight of her parents' sadness at dismantling their beautiful shop.

But the new version would be beautiful too. Her mother had the decorative gene, which had made the shop look like a quaint and cozy gift cottage. Now it would simply morph into a quaint and cozy cookie cottage.

"Mom, how about changing the name to Barb's Cookie Cottage? It's not a major difference, and you need to brand it to let the public know what you're selling."

Her mother continued wrapping her wares in tissue paper before packing them gently into the designated boxes. "That's fine."

But no joy emerged from this new venture.

"I know today is difficult. But once we get all this packed and stored and transform the shop for its new operation, I'm sure you'll feel better."

At least she hoped so. She didn't want to be the reason her parents, and especially her mom, fell into a deep depression. Not that she was the initial cause of the shop's downward spiral, but she couldn't help feeling that her push for change was too much, too soon. Although in all probability, it was too little, too late.

As they were packing the last box, as if by telepathy, Dean and crew showed up. Her dad must have texted him a while back, giving him the estimated time of arrival. *Such in-sync friends.* She rolled her eyes for the mere purpose of making herself feel better.

This was her cue to exit. She'd go back to the house, thereby eliminating any interactions with Dean, and work on the marketing plan in peace. Her first item of attack was to set up a website. And now that she had her mother's lukewarm agreement to change the name of the business, along with a list of cookies which names she could easily neutralize, she could tackle the job.

Her undergraduate minor in marketing would finally

come in handy.

****

Dean had been waiting all day to get the call from Clive. Not that he couldn't wait to rearrange furniture and cases in the gift shop, but because his blood pumped every time he thought of Bella. The combination of excitement and dread had him confused.

She was such a presence! Beautiful—with thick, dark hair that his fingers itched to comb through, flashing blue eyes that sucked him in, and a tall, lithe body that somehow looked good in flannel pajamas. Although he'd rather see her in silk and lace.

On more than one occasion today, he'd gotten lost in the memory of her standing on the ladder, her arms overhead, sweater inching up to give him an eyeful of her soft, silky midriff. When she leaned over too far, he'd slid his palms around her waist in an attempt to keep her from falling. At least that's the excuse he'd used.

He'd like to be back there right now, just the two of them, working together, brushing against each other, eliciting fireworks that went straight to his core.

But even more than her lovely assets, he was mesmerized by her powerful energy in taking charge of a problem and working to find answers. She didn't force anything. She collaborated. All while steering her stubborn audience toward her resolutions.

Despite his captivation with her, she unfortunately didn't hold him in like esteem. She'd disregarded his inquiry into the cause of her clear disturbance over his presence by closing down and refusing to discuss it. Of course, it hadn't helped matters when he sided with her parents last night about not changing the store. With the exception of a thirty-second interlude where they'd connected on some other level, her eye daggers and ice-cold voice had been lethal.

And today, despite Clive and Barb's change of heart and his willingness to help out with whatever they wanted to do, her steely glance told him he was not forgiven for his opinion last night and whatever other grievance she had against him.

With luck, he'd be able to steer her to a remote corner of the store today while they were rearranging, to attempt to get on her better side. At least, that was the plan.

"I'll see you later, Mom and Dad. It looks like you have enough help here. I'm going home to work on the website." She grabbed her coat and headed for the door.

He intercepted. "Bella." He slipped his hand over her wrist, and his fingers burned with electrified currents. "Wait. I…I want to apologize for last night. You were right. It wasn't my place to express my opinion about the shop." He swallowed his angst, hoping his words would melt the iciness still present in her sapphire eyes. "I'm used to having discussions with your folks. They like to run things by me. But now that you're here, I'll step back."

He tried to conncct with her gaze, to let her see how truly sorry he was, and that he meant what he said. But she glanced past him.

"Okay." She pulled her hand out of his grasp. "I need to get going."

"Wait." A gut-deep need pushed him to come up with something, anything to make her stay. "Don't you want to make sure we move all the furniture to the right place? The guys from the nursery and I only have an hour before we have to be back to unload a shipment."

Keying in to Bella's craving to control while putting a time limit on his presence might convince her to reconsider. In his eyes, any interval, no matter how short, would give him an opportunity to dig away at her barriers and inch into her psyche. He'd pull out all the stops—humor, kindness, flirting. Whatever it took to be the beneficiary of that smile.

She turned away, tossing her answer over her shoulder. "Just follow the diagram. It's clear enough."

And with that, she was out the door, shutting down his plot to dazzle her.

No opportunity for humor, kindness, or flirting. And definitely no smile.

So much for working his way into Bella's good graces.

Chapter Seven

For the next two weeks leading up to the grand reopening of Barb's Cookie Cottage, Bella, her parents, and their favored child, Dean, readied the store for their new venture. Bella tried hard to avoid the man who selflessly gave of his time to do her parents' bidding— even at a moment's notice. Whenever he neared, her internal radar announced his presence, and pleasurable shivers ran through her system. His good humor and ready smile, directed at her, sent her heart spiraling.

In order to keep him from inching further into her bloodstream, she erected blocks. Whenever possible, she left the shop upon his arrival, as if working on the next steps of her marketing plan could only be done from her parents' house. But there were times when he'd prevent her furtive escape with a warm hand that caressed her wrist while he seduced her with his sincere request that she stay. And those were the times she couldn't strip from her mind. Just his nearness sent her heartbeat into overdrive as it pounded against her ribs. Her entire body flushed with the heat of desire. And the way he looked at her—like he wanted to rip off her clothes and ravish her. *Oh my.*

These reactions were all the more reason to dodge him at every turn. They clearly weren't going to start dating. His coldheartedness and insensitivity from years before wouldn't simply disappear from her memory, even if he had buried them. Besides, she'd be back in New York City in a little over a month, slaving away at her next job, and he'd be here in Princeton, doing his landscape architect thing. They'd live the lives they'd been living, untouched by the other's existence.

Frustration, angst, and desire stirred within at this untenable situation. She needed to walk it off. "Mom, I'm going to distribute these. I'll be back."

Bella had created a flier and stopped at every store in town, asking if she could put it in their window to advertise their grand reopening as well as their new branding. Since the community was so warm and supportive, no one denied her request.

On the day of the unveiling, four display cases filled with buttery, sugary cookies lined the right side of the store, radiating an aroma to die for. The bookcases behind them were decorated with stuffed bears, elves, Santas, and nutcrackers along with colorful holiday tins to purchase and fill with cookies as gifts.

A brand-new coffee machine, which also produced tea or hot chocolate, sat at the back end of the bookcases. Several tables were covered with Christmas themed cloths, and eclectic caned chairs accompanied them—all set up between the window and the middle of the store on the left side. The back of the store held their Christmas tree, still decorated with jewelry, scarves, and ornamental Christmas balls for purchase, as well as two tables of specially selected gifts for the season.

The event was a success!

A steady stream of customers kept them running from morning till night. But the best thing about the day was witnessing the joy in her parents' eyes over the effective transition.

Regrettably, the momentum of that day couldn't be duplicated on just any given day. Sure, they had customers, more customers than they'd had in a while. And the community seemed to really enjoy the new gathering space.

Bella sat before her laptop at one of the empty tables in the shop window, adding some information to the website—a work in progress. It already contained the history of the store—along with its new branding—and provided plenty of photos to show the public how beautiful the cottage was in its new iteration. It also had an e-store section with photos of the hand-crafted wares that were for sale through the site.

"Look what came in the mail." Her dad appeared from his office in the back, his hazel eyes grim and his salt-and-pepper hair sticking up as if gelled—which was not the case.

"What is it, Clive?" asked her mom as she added more cookies to the case.

"A tax sale notice." His gaze darted to Bella, panic in their depths. "Can you take a look at this?" He handed her the letter, a tremor in his hand.

"Calm down, Dad. We can fix this." She kept her voice calm and measured, aiming to stave off his fear before her mother took it on and added to the alarm.

She quickly read the notice, familiar with tax sales from practicing law. "Since you owe taxes on the shop, the municipality of Princeton has the right to hold a sale of the unpaid taxes. This notice tells you the date of the tax sale, which is January thirtieth. The highest bidder at the sale pays the outstanding taxes and becomes the holder of a tax sale certificate. That person does not own the property." She looked at her parents to make sure what she said was sinking in. "He or she owns a lien against the property for the amount of taxes paid plus interest. You can pay off the taxes you owe even after the tax sale."

Her mom's ashen face told her she hadn't quite alleviated her fear.

"We need to find that money right now, Clive. We can't have someone holding a lien over our heads."

"We don't have the money, Barb." Her dad's defeated tone matched his slumped shoulders. "Bella, can we lose the property?"

"No!" She hadn't meant to sound so forceful, but she needed to waylay their distress. "The person who holds the tax sale certificate by paying the taxes has a right to foreclose upon the property, but only after two years. You'll have plenty of time to come up with the money."

Of course, they'd need to keep all future taxes current as well and pay all their other bills. She now worried the foot traffic for coffee and cookies, although much more than before, was not going to keep the store afloat.

Warrior mode was necessary. "We implemented the first part of the plan to change the focus of the shop. But we have to do more. We need to market to people out of the area, out of state, who we could then ship cookies to."

Her parents gained some of their color back and were now staring at her with mouths agape as if she were speaking a foreign language.

"Mom. What do you think about posting a video of you making one of your favorite Christmas cookies on social media?"

"Why would anyone want to watch that?"

"I don't know why *anyone* watches cooking or baking shows, but they do." Bella had survived on take-out in New York and had no wish to learn any culinary skills. "Maybe we can figure out a way to make it funny."

"I'm not a comedian," her mother stated, as if Bella didn't know that. "And I don't want to be filmed. It would make me nervous."

While her mother was friendly to her customers, Bella understood that talking one-on-one with someone was much different than talking to a camera. Even if Bella was behind the camera.

"How about if you teach someone how to make the cookies on a video? One of your friends. Perhaps it would be easier if you were actually showing another person. That could work, right?"

Her mother rolled her eyes. "It would be frustrating and take too long."

"You can't do it with that attitude. You'd have to cooperate, knowing the video would be posted on YouTube or TikTok as a way to get customers."

"Why don't we advertise in the newspaper instead?"

"Because a lot of people don't read the newspaper. They get their news online. And it would be expensive. This would be free. Either Dad or I could video it."

"I don't know…"

At least her mom was softening. "I'll do some research, watch other videos, and come up with a plan. You figure out what cookie you want to do first. It should be something that will become your signature cookie— what everyone comes here to get."

"That's easy. It's my red velvet crinkles."

"What are they? You never made them when I was little."

"I've been adding to my repertoire for years. If you'd been around more, you would know about all the different cookies I've been making."

"Okay, okay. I've been busy going to school and then working."

"Well, red velvet crinkles have dark chocolate, white chocolate, sugar, butter, eggs, vanilla, flour, and red food coloring."

"Other than the red food coloring, those ingredients are similar to those in every other cookie, no?"

"Yes, but the deliciousness is in the proportions. And of course, the love that goes into baking them."

"Is it easy enough to teach someone how to make them? Would I be able to learn?"

Her mother raised her brows. "All cookies are easy to make. But you need to have the will to want to make them. You've never been that good at it. If I asked you for a cup of flour, you would use the liquid measure instead of the dry measuring cups."

"What difference does that make? A cup is a cup."

"You see? No patience for doing it right."

The wheels started to turn in her head. "What if I helped you in the video and did everything wrong? Those would be good teaching moments to your viewers, and they could be funny. Maybe."

"Maybe." Her mom did not sound convinced, and frankly neither was she.

But if they didn't come up with something to get the word out to a larger clientele, this venture would fail. And she was too stubborn to let that happen.

"Hey, Barb, how's it going? Hi, Bella."

Dean's voice echoed around her before hitting the spot in her stomach where it whirled, making her gooey.

Traitor.

"Hi, Dean," her mother responded. "You're just in time for this discussion."

Bella shook her head. Nothing could ever be merely between her and her parents. Dean always had to be included.

"What discussion is that?"

"Bella wants us to do a video for Tick Tack or something, where I teach her how to bake cookies."

A laugh escaped. "Bella, you can't bake."

"How do you know?" she huffed.

"Anytime you made cookies when we were in high school, they were kind of dry and crumbly."

"That's because Bella doesn't know the difference between wet and dry measures."

She threw her hands up. "I can't believe this."

Her mom continued. "Bella thinks we need to spread a wider net, to get customers from out of town. Of course, that would mean we'd have to start shipping cookies, but I'm sure we could figure that out if need be."

Dean nodded. "There's that bakery in Cobblestone Village that has a huge following. I know they ship. Bella, do you want to take a ride with me to go check it out? Maybe we can talk to the owner and find out how they got to where they are in sales."

"I'm sure they'd want to pass along their marketing ideas to us."

He adeptly sidestepped her sarcasm. "They're about forty-five minutes away, a little past New Hope. It's not like you would be direct competition with them. I'll drive, and on the way, you could check out their website. Maybe shoot them an email or call to see if they'll talk to you."

"That would be wonderful," her mom squealed.

Of course, every idea Dean had was wonderful while every idea she had came with an argument.

While she'd managed to evade Dean over the past few weeks, usually finding something to do in the storeroom or the kitchen or back home when he showed up, his skillful collusion with her mom was making it impossible to get out of this one. After all, this whole cookie business had been her idea. She should check out, in person, what a similar business did to succeed.

"O…kay. Let's go." Her halfhearted response couldn't be missed.

She'd simply ignore Dean on the drive by studying the shop's website.

The sun shone brightly as they crossed the Delaware River into Pennsylvania, and Bella wasn't following her own rule of keeping her eyes glued to her phone. Instead, she enjoyed the scenery—the sparkling water dancing over the rocks of the river bed, the houses from the 1800s hugging the road. Websites were the furthest from her mind.

"I'm glad I finally have you to myself."

His words sent flashes of heat from her toes to her head. She glanced over at him, and his face was unexpectedly vulnerable.

"I'd like to discuss the reason you keep avoiding me."

An uneasy chuckle escaped. "I'm hardly avoiding you. You're always around."

"You sound annoyed by that. Why? Please tell me what I've done to offend you."

She could find no way around this discussion. He had her trapped in a car with a half hour to go before reaching their destination. Besides, she should air her grievances. She'd been carrying around this resentment for way too many years, and if she didn't deal with it, she'd be harboring these same destructive feelings for the next month.

She cloaked herself in courage. "I know it's been years, and my upset over the past should have been put to rest, but it's not." She paused, considering whether that sentence made sense. "Resting, that is. My upset is not resting." She shook her head, admonishing herself to get to the point. "The way you treated me when we were in high school is something I can't forget. Your callousness was hurtful and cruel."

"You mean when I teased you?"

Did he not remember it was much more than that? "That was part of it." Her face heated, and she was sure her cheeks blazed red. "Do you remember that I invited you to my junior prom?"

His jaw tightened, so she took that as a yes but continued to set the scene.

"You were at one of the parties my brother had at our house, and there were a lot of kids around. I thought no one would notice if I pulled you aside. That was the hardest conversation I ever had back then. I was so nervous, and although I was fairly certain you'd say no, I was still hopeful." She swallowed, her mouth as dry as fake snow. "You shocked me, in a good way, when you agreed to go. I was so happy, floating around for the next two weeks. I bought a beautiful gown and told my friends I had a date. Thankfully, I had kept it a secret who I was going with. I guess in the back of my mind, I was afraid to jinx it."

She glanced over at him, but he stared ahead at the

road.

"Then you called and cancelled a few days before. No explanation other than you couldn't make it." Tears stung the backs of her eyes as she relived that awful phone conversation. Her throat had been so tight she couldn't respond. Even now she suffered the cutting pain as if he had said those very words today.

He reached out to take her hand, but she pulled it away.

"Bella, I am so, so sorry. I do remember that." He exhaled. "I actually wanted to go with you, but soon after I'd agreed, Scott made it clear to all us guys that we were to stay away from his little sister. I assumed he knew you had asked me to go to the prom, and he was speaking directly to me. But he didn't single me out. He said that if any of us so much as looked at you, our friendship would be over. No one wanted to mess with that. Me included. We were all on the football team, best of friends. Loyalty mattered."

He glanced over at her, and his eyes looked glassy. Or was that just the reflection from the sun streaming through the bare tree branches?

"I didn't mean to hurt you. I cancelled as soon as Scott made his pronouncement."

"You not only hurt me; you stomped on my self-esteem. It had taken a lot to feel good about myself to even ask you. Up until that year, I'd felt invisible for the most part—or if I was seen, I was teased. My junior year had been a time of transformation. No more glasses, the braces were gone, ballet had boosted my confidence in my body, and I had made it onto the debate team."

"You were the only junior on the team if I'm not mistaken. And you won the trophy that year."

She smiled at the memory as well as the fact that he recalled it. But in seconds, she sobered. "I thought you had noticed me. Every once in a while, when we were in the store together, you would talk to me, just me. And you'd look at me like…" Like what? To a sixteen-year-old who had never had a boyfriend, what did his stares mean? "I don't know." She sighed. "Yet you canceled our date as if it were nothing."

The air in the car hung heavy around her. She shouldn't have started this conversation when she couldn't get away.

His voice was strained, contrite. "I should have been more of a grown-up about it and told you what had happened. Or I should have gone with you and tossed aside Scott's threats. But I was immature, and my friendships meant more to me than they should have. I believed Scott would have cut me off. As it was, he had caught me staring at you a few times, especially when we were in the store together, and gave me the evil eye." He shook his head. "Once you turned sixteen, you were no longer a little girl with glasses, pigtails, and sweatshirts. You were beautiful, and I was infatuated. But you were off-limits."

Why hadn't she known that Scott was acting the caveman brother? "He had no right to do that." Her voice came out raspy, rough.

"He was trying to protect you from the likes of us. All we wanted to do back then was to see how far we could get sexually with girls. We were popular and full of confidence and bravado. We were idiots."

That made her smile. She finally met his eyes. "Yes, you were." Some of the angst dissipated, and in its place understanding shone through, an emotion she hadn't experienced since before he walked into her parents' kitchen that first morning. But she wasn't finished. "I was ecstatic when you went off to college so I no longer had to come face-to-face with the person who had humiliated me."

"Ouch." He sighed, his jaw clenching as if punched. "Bella, I never knew I had hurt you so deeply. You were so pretty I thought you'd get another date in a flash. I'm very sorry. If I could go back and change things, I would."

This time when he took her hand, she let him, allowing his warmth to swirl through her along with his sincere apology.

She exhaled the past and all the pent-up anger that had surfaced in seeing him for the first time in years. His explanation seemed genuine. Her brother had always been protective of her, although she hadn't known the extent. She needed to let this go.

Not only did all this happen a lifetime ago, but he'd been an amazing help to her parents throughout their business transformation and before. And here he was driving her to Cobblestone Village to support her marketing ideas as if he had nothing better to do.

"Apology accepted." She glanced at him as he drove, and couldn't miss the trace of relief that washed through those beautiful eyes. "I felt foolish bringing it up since it happened so long ago. But slights we receive as vulnerable teenagers never truly go away."

Hopefully now she could look at him in a different light and not scowl, frown, and cast verbal darts when he appeared as often as he did, given the relationship he'd developed with her parents. And the cordial friendship he seemed to want to develop with her.

"Are you sure we're okay?"

His gentle voice and caressing words melted the ice she had placed around her heart.

"I'm sure."

Chapter Eight

Their outing had been a success personally. Now if only the good vibes could continue as they followed their path to Ye Olde Village Bakery, Dean would be ecstatic. When they arrived at their destination, the bakery was swarming with a line out the door on a Tuesday afternoon, proving its success. Bella engaged with the owner who was only too happy to show off and boast about her incredible shop.

Of course, the entire village, with dozens of stores and several restaurants, was a draw. A million colorful lights wound around tree trunks and limbs, outlined roofs and eaves, and created tunnels over several walkways. The Gingerbread House Competition and Display was set in a festive barn where over eighty structures of intricate, imaginative, and artsy contenders vied for that first-place ribbon. In his view, they all deserved an award, not only for their creativity, but for the sweet smell of ginger, sugar, and cinnamon that permeated the air. This was a magical place.

Dean convinced Bella to walk around the village with him to see if any other shops caught her eye. In reality, he simply wanted to spend time with her now that she had accepted his apology for being such a fool when they were younger. Perhaps they could now reconnect as adults, because he would sure like to entertain some of those teenage fantasies in real life.

"You haven't said much about quitting your job in New York. I was surprised you'd do that without having another job lined up." Although he wasn't touching her, he could feel the tension vibrate between them.

"I didn't exactly quit." She kept her gaze straight ahead, and her cheeks flamed red. "I was…let go."

"Oh. I'm sorry." He wanted to reach out and draw her into his embrace, but they'd only just repaired their relationship. Comfort might not be what she wanted from him. "Do you want to talk about it?"

She shrugged. "I haven't even told my parents that truth. It's incredibly embarrassing to get fired. To them I've always been their brilliant daughter who went to an Ivy League college and law school, who got a top-notch job at a New York City law firm. Who was on her way up the ladder of success. Now look at me. Out of work, homeless."

This was much heavier than he'd thought. He steered her to a bench, and he sat facing her. "What happened?"

Silence took up residence between them. She eventually nodded, her eyes shiny with unshed tears. "There's not much to say. The recession hit law firms hard. The partners decided to lay off twenty percent of their attorneys. I was one of them, despite the fact I had brought in two major clients. They'd been thrilled with me—an up-and-coming superstar. And I was one of the highest billing associates. I don't understand how I ended up in the twenty-percent group."

"With your credentials, you should be able to get another job quickly."

In high school, she had gotten straight As, then she'd gone to Yale for her undergraduate degree and Columbia for her law degree. With all that, plus over three years working at a major New York City firm, how could she not be scooped up?

"No one is hiring now. They're all letting lawyers go. In January, I'll be one of thousands vying for any available job." She sighed. "It's not like I loved my job. The hours were incredibly long, and although I learned a lot about corporate structure and tax issues, my efforts were solitary and tedious most of the time. But I had worked so hard to get there. To be let go is mortifying."

"It wasn't your fault. Your firm made a bottom-line decision, and you unfortunately happened to be a casualty of lower profits."

"Said like a true businessman."

He stood and pulled her up with him. "You were right to come home. Give it a break. Let it all go. After the new year, you can start fresh and decide on your plan of attack." Throwing caution to the wind, he pulled her into a hug, attempting to transfer some of her angst to him. "I'll be here for you whenever you need me. If you just want to talk, I'll listen. If you want to strategize, I'm at your service."

Her arms reached around him, and she hugged him back, shooting off cherry bombs near his heart.

"Thanks, Dean. Talking about it has helped."

She pulled away and looked up at him, her deep blue eyes clearer, less sad than they were before her confession. He could get lost in those depths.

"You're a good friend. Not only to my parents and to Scott. But to me."

Friends. Disappointment swirled through his veins.

He'd have to do something drastic to get himself out of that category.

****

The sun had set, and the sky darkened to an inky black as hundreds of stars twinkled above.

"That pulled-pork sandwich was amazing." Bella had practically inhaled her dinner at the Pig and Poke, a barbecue restaurant on the fringe of the village. "I was so hungry, if we didn't get out of there, I might have ordered another one."

"Why didn't you? I would have enjoyed watching."

His smile warmed her inside and out. If she wasn't careful, she'd fall right back into the abyss of her high school crush.

Today had been a momentous day between them. She'd gotten over her injured ego from high school, shared the painful story of being fired from her job, and fallen into an easy camaraderie with the man she'd been trying to ignore. As if that weren't enough, she'd gotten helpful information from the owner of Ye Olde Village Bakery on the cookie business.

"It's time to get back." She tugged on Dean's arm to hurry him along. "I have work to do on the marketing plan for my parents."

"It's seven o'clock. We won't get home until eight. I'm sure it can wait until tomorrow."

"I'm used to working twelve-hour days. And all these ideas are bouncing around in my head. I need to get them down on paper."

They followed the cobblestone walkway that would take them to the other side of the village where the car was parked.

He directed her toward the longer route. "How about some hot chocolate? I saw a coffee shop on our way to the restaurant down this way."

She stopped short. "Are you trying to interfere with my creativity?"

He moved in front of her, placing his hands on her upper arms, inching farther into her space. "I'm trying to curb your workaholic ways. You need to have fun sometimes. It appears that it has been missing from your life for quite a while."

His smile turned serious, and his emerald eyes darkened, searching hers as if asking a question. But no words came out as his mouth edged closer, their breath mingling, before his lips whispered a kiss across hers. A delicious dizziness took hold, and she snaked her arms around his neck as her eyes closed. Anticipation buzzed in her core. She could feel his heat, his electric current, surround her, but his mouth was absent.

She lifted her lids. He was an inch away, studying her.

Her gloved hand caressed his cheek, his jaw, as she remained under the power of his gaze. But she craved more. Required more. Reaching up, she connected with his lips, a slow sensual dance at first, until he covered her mouth with his, their chaste kiss turning hot and steamy. His hands settled against her back, and he pulled her closer, but their winter coats refused to allow their bodies to touch.

Despite being outside in thirty-degree weather, despite the people milling about the village bypassing them, Bella could have stayed there forever. The boy who had taken over her teenage dreams was now the man in her arms, and she never wanted this kiss, this connection to end.

"Hey, get a room." A teen's laughter amongst his friends had Bella jumping back.

Then Dean started laughing too, before sobering. "He's right. That's something we'll have to discuss. Perhaps in the car ride home."

He took her hand and tugged her in the direction of the parking lot, as her stomach tumbled and rolled—in a good way.

When one door closed, another one opened.

Chapter Nine

He shouldn't push. They had finally gotten to a better place in their relationship. He needed to take it slow, make sure Bella was on the same page. He'd known he wanted her since that night in her parents' kitchen when she dared him, with those flashing eyes, to come up with a better plan than hers for the shop. She was a fighter and a problem solver but also a mediator. It had been three against one that night, but she came up the winner.

Ever since that night he'd schemed to be around her, hoping she'd drop the armor she wore to fend him off. But while he put himself in her direct path, she'd deftly evaded him, all while making it seem practical.

Until today. The opportunity presented itself, and he pounced on the prospect of having her to himself. After a rocky start, it had worked. They'd talked things out, shared pieces of themselves, and kissed—a hot, sensual, heart-thumping kiss that he wouldn't soon forget. She had to feel it too.

Yet he questioned his ability to read her. If he put it all out there and shared his feelings, would she hand his heart back to him with a "thanks but no thanks"? Her disregard for him over this past month had knocked him down more than a few pegs on the confidence ladder. With any luck, their conversation today, clearing the air over his idiotic treatment of her in high school, would pave the road for a steamy romance.

He cranked up the heat as soon as he started the car. "There's a blanket in the back if you want it."

"I'm fine, thanks. I'm used to the cold of New York City. The wind whipping around corners, freezing my face and fingers, despite gloves." She rubbed her hands together to warm them.

"You were always drawn to the city. Why?"

"At first, I wanted to get away from home. Go someplace where I'd be accepted more." She paused before glancing in his direction. "It wasn't only you and your posse who teased me."

He swallowed his embarrassment. "Kids could be so cruel. And I know I was no angel. But you had friends. Life couldn't have been all bad."

"It probably wasn't. When you're going through those trying times, things seem worse. It didn't help that Scott was extremely popular and brought home all those kids from the group that I wanted to be a part of. I wasn't invited, and when I did show up, sticking close to the wall or moving around to stay out of Scott's sight, I was invisible to the rest of you. I wanted to go to a place where I'd be seen."

"You weren't unnoticed, Bella. The guys from the team, including me, definitely saw you. But Scott had us by the collar."

"I'm going to have to have a talk with him." She chuckled.

"Despite high school angst, you managed to shine bright." He, for one, was becoming blinded by her sparkle. "Did you leave your Mr. Right behind in the city?"

That generated a full-blown laugh. "You'd think

with all the single men there, I would have found him. But work took over my life. What little free time I had, I selfishly wanted to myself." She quickly added, "Although I did go on dates here and there. No one special, though." Sadness tinged her voice. "What about you? I heard on one of my trips home that you were hot and heavy with someone."

"I was. At first. But she had a nine-to-five job with weekends off and wanted to spend every one of her free hours with me. In the beginning, I was flattered. But eventually, it became suffocating. She was not what I was looking for."

"I'm sorry it didn't work out."

He hoped she was saying that to be nice and didn't really mean it.

She continued. "What is it you're looking for?"

"Someone independent, hardworking, smart." He was describing Bella to a T, although she probably wouldn't see it.

"There are thousands of women like that in New York City. Maybe you should relocate."

While New York City was fun to visit, he wasn't at all sure he could live there. And it didn't seem as if she was suggesting it because she wanted to be with him. Rather, she was giving him advice on where to meet other women.

"When are you going back?" He held his breath.

"As soon as I find a job. I hired a headhunter who advised me to wait until the new year to start a search in earnest. Hopefully, the economy will change for the better."

"Did you ever consider moving back here to work? There are plenty of law firms in the area. Or you could open your own practice."

Her laugh, although musical, disappointed him.

"No. I left small-town life behind when I went to law school in New York City. I wanted to make it in the financial capital of the world."

"And you did. You have nothing more to prove."

The tires on the road were the only sound that broke through their silence following his truthful statement. Maybe she was considering it. Maybe not.

She exhaled. "Let's talk about you."

"Me? What about me?"

"How did you end up back here? As I recall, you had a football scholarship to Florida State."

"I got hurt my third year, which destroyed any hope of making it to the pros. Probably a good thing, since I was one of thousands dreaming that fantasy. Once my football career was over, I dove headfirst into my major, landscape architecture, and continued on to get a master's degree. I had planned to stay in Florida where the weather is nice year round so my job wouldn't be affected in the winter months."

"If you wanted to stay in Florida, what brought you back?"

"My dad's nursery business was struggling, and although my brother was helping him, it was still failing. I tried giving advice from afar, but it didn't work. My father was getting more and more depressed—with bankruptcy hanging over his head—so I came back." He glanced over at her. "My move was meant to be temporary, but I put in a lot of time and effort to start my own landscape architecture business, which was attached to the nursery. That really helped my dad's business since I used the nursery's shrubs, trees, and flowers for my designs. Now both businesses are thriving." His pleasure was tinged with sadness. "I was glad my dad lived long enough to see the success of it all. Even so, he died too soon."

She took his hand and squeezed it. "I know how close you were to your dad. Especially after your mom died. I'm really sorry."

"Thanks." Sorrow welled within at the untimely deaths of both his parents. Yet he savored her fingers threaded through his as a silent moment of remembrance connected them further.

"How did you start getting business when you first moved up here?"

He grinned to himself. The ever workaholic was now transitioning into business mode for her parents' shop.

"Initially, I got residential jobs, which came in through the nursery. But I realized early on it would be more lucrative to design parks, gardens, and other large public and private areas. In my spare time, I drove up and down the major thoroughfares from Lawrenceville to New Brunswick and over to Somerville, looking at corporate campuses, prep schools, colleges, and parks. I made a list of those I thought I could spruce up, then did a lot of research online, trying to figure out how to connect with the right people. I decided that dealing with municipalities might be a good start, since they were in charge of their parks and public schools. The process was slow at first, but once I had a few behind me, I was able to leverage them into bigger and better jobs. My business grew to college campuses, then corporate campuses. There are dozens around here on and off the Route 1 corridor. It's no longer difficult to find jobs."

"Because of your reputation."

"Yes."

He could almost see the synapses of her brain firing. Her lips moved, as if she were talking to herself.

"What are you thinking?" he finally asked.

"I might be able to use the same idea with my parents' business. I could make a list of all the corporations in the area, put together a proposal for corporate or employee gifts, and if they order, save on mailing costs by delivering them myself."

"Or you could hire a college student, who could use a little extra cash around the holidays, to do the deliveries for you. You can't do everything, Bella."

She smiled. "You're right. I have this problem with delegating. I always think I could do it better."

They were almost home, and a strange, disheartening melancholy pressed on his chest. Today had been an extraordinary day, for he had gotten to know her on a deeper level. His attraction to her flew off the charts.

Bella was the one who could make his life perfect. She was independent, strong, smart. And loyal to her family. The person he was looking for.

Now all he had to do was convince her that she was looking for him.

Chapter Ten

Dean was a genius. She'd have to tell him that if she ever came up for air.

Bella worked tirelessly over the next few weeks, at first designing a pamphlet, having them printed—at a cost she absorbed with the last of her savings—then dropping them off to those in charge of gift-giving at various corporations, banks, law firms, accountants' offices, and whatever else caught her eye. Samples helped, and she never failed to give whomever would speak to her a small box of her mom's favorite—red velvet crinkles.

A few mornings, she would help her mom bake cookies, and her dad would video their interchange. Usually with her mom directing her to measure some ingredient and telling her it needed to be precise, not an approximation as Bella was wont to do.

Their conversation would go something like:

"Bella, could you please get the baking powder and add one tablespoon to these dry ingredients?"

"Sure, Mom." Then she'd pick up the baking soda.

"Not baking soda. Baking powder."

"What's the difference?"

"Is there a difference in the law between libel and slander?"

"Of course. What does that have to do with anything?" Bella frowned to let her mom and the potential viewers know that baking powder and libel were mutually exclusive.

"As a lawyer, I'm sure you wouldn't confuse the two."

"Of course not. You need to prove different elements."

"Baking powder and baking soda have different elements. If you use baking soda—which always requires less than baking powder and is used in conjunction with certain ingredients to form a reaction— you will most assuredly have leftover baking soda in the recipe, which creates a metallic, soapy taste in your baked goods. Is that what you want?"

She would then sheepishly smile and produce the correct ingredient, with her mom looking over her shoulder to make sure she was now following directions.

"That's too much. I said a tablespoon."

"This is a tablespoon."

"It's not level. There's a mound."

"Jeesh." Bella would then get a knife and level off the "mound."

They did several of these videos, with Bella poring through online articles on baking mistakes just so she could make them, allowing her mother to educate her.

Who knew there was a proper technique for measuring flour? Apparently, one spooned it into the measuring cup instead of dipping into the flour bag, because no one wanted excess flour causing a crumbly cookie. And too much sugar made cookies brittle. One wouldn't want others to break their teeth on oversweetened bakery items. Not thoroughly creaming the butter and sugar resulted in flat, dense cookies instead of the more appealing light and fluffy ones. Not chilling the dough when called for meant the batter would spread quickly and aggressively once in the oven. Presumably no one wanted an aggressive cookie.

And the mortal sin of baking—using liquid measuring cups to measure dry ingredients. Or vice versa. So much to learn.

While Bella loved doing the research and coming up with the witty repartee, she didn't fancy being the foolish, naïve student to her mother's superior talents. They'd have to find another stooge soon.

Although she had to take some credit. More and more people were clicking onto their videos, which in turn generated more and more orders.

Dean had texted her a few times, asking if she'd like to get together for dinner, and although she would have loved to accept his invitation, right now she didn't have any time to give. At least, that's the excuse she used. There could be no rational reason for getting closer to the man who made her pulse race merely at the thought of that scorching kiss—a thought that invaded her daydreams and night dreams far too often.

Even now her stomach swirled, and tiny flapping wings tickled her heart.

She had to put an end to this craziness. Christmas was next week, and time was of the essence to reel in as many customers, including local companies, as possible. Not only would it help tremendously with the bottom line at the end of the year, but it could potentially give the shop the boost it needed to move into next year. Because of course, once these newbies tasted her mom's cookies, she had no doubt they'd be customers for life.

Both of her ideas were working. Orders were pouring in, especially for red velvet crinkles. Every night after the shop closed, she helped her mom bake and fill the orders they'd gotten that day. In the morning, they'd continue baking, box and ship what needed to be mailed, and prepare the orders that could be hand delivered. She had taken Dean's advice and hired a responsible college kid to help with deliveries, but she kept the major clients on her route, making sure they knew different cookies would be available every month.

As she headed to her mom's car, going over the schedule for deliveries in her head, a hand wound around her arm, sending tingles and electric pops through her bloodstream.

"Bella, wait a sec."

His warm voice curled through her system and ribboned her heart. "Dean. Hi." She locked gazes with him, and the deep pools of green sucked her in.

"I know you've been busy helping your parents, but the Christmas gala is coming up. You're going, right?"

She dragged her gaze from his, kicking and screaming. "My parents bought three tickets, but I haven't committed yet. I might want to stay in and collapse on Saturday night."

"You have to come. It's the event of the season. It will be fun."

Interestingly, he didn't invite her to go with him. Perhaps all her rejections of his dinner invitations had finally worn him down. Guarding her heart was a double-edged sword as uncalled-for disappointment kicked her in the gut.

She swallowed the swirling dread and excitement rolled into one.

How could one little Christmas gala hurt?

****

110

"Are you ready to go to the gala, Bella?" Her mother knocked on her bedroom door.

On the Saturday before Christmas, for every year since she could remember, her parents went to support whatever charity the town had voted on to help. The nonprofit receiving the funds this year was Homefront, an organization that aided the homeless in Central New Jersey by providing meals, emergency shelter, back rent, utility assistance, clothing, household goods, and job placement skills. Bella had volunteered for the organization when she was in high school. While she had toyed with staying in and relaxing tonight, when it came right down to it, she knew she'd go.

Especially since Dean would be there. She'd learned he was on the committee in charge of silent-auction items when he'd asked her and her parents to donate. Her parents supplied three baskets of cookies, with each basket containing different varieties and a gift certificate. After much arm-twisting, she had donated a custom business plan. Not that she didn't want to contribute to the event, but she merely couldn't imagine anyone bidding on such a thing—especially from her.

When they arrived at the Hyatt, her father surprisingly entered the valet line instead of stubbornly heading for the self-parking area.

"Clive, that's so nice of you to not make us walk a quarter mile in heels tonight." Her mom smiled at her dad.

"I saw those spikey heels Bella was wearing and knew she wouldn't make it." He turned toward the back seat and gave her a wink.

"Thanks, Dad. That's nice of you."

She no longer felt like a kid in her parents'

presence—despite being relegated to the back seat. They had bitten the bullet and courageously followed every suggestion of her business plan, finally relying on her expertise to guide them.

The lobby of the motel as well as the reception area had been turned into a winter wonderland, with fake trees holding snow, dripping icicles, and sparkling with the radiance of thousands of twinkling white lights.

She surreptitiously searched for Dean, wondering if he would have a date by his side. After all, this was a formal affair on a Saturday night, and she had been ambivalent about whether she would attend.

After scanning the area once again for the man who robbed her of breath, she perused the items on the silent-auction tables. She would do her part and bid on a few to contribute to this worthwhile cause.

Her mom's cookie baskets were already generating bids, which moved on to the second page and had topped four hundred dollars. The generosity of the townspeople was amazing.

Right next to one of the cookie baskets was her donation. A very nice description of her service along with her bio and professional photo—who had given Dean that?—were placed above the bidding sheet. She squinted her eyes, almost closing them, before peeking at the sheet. Instead of an empty page, as she suspected, her donation had also garnered dozens of bids. And the bid was up to five thousand five hundred dollars. *What?*

A warm hand caressed her hip, and the sensual scent of sandalwood and leather tickled her nose before she could see his handsome face.

"Hi, Bella."

His greeting whispered near her ear and sent a thrill

cascading straight through to her core. She turned, and Dean stood within inches, dressed in a tuxedo that had to be custom made—its fit perfect.

"I love the suit," she managed.

"You look amazing." He stood back a step and took her in. "Red is your color."

Her stomach spun and fizzed as if in its own Jacuzzi.

She had chosen a red clingy gown with one shoulder bare and a long slit up her leg. If she had thought about it too long, she would have acknowledged she had dressed to entice Dean despite her admonition to stay away.

"Thank you. You've done a great job with this auction. People are bidding high."

"It's because of the quality of the items." A huge smile covered those kissable lips. "I'm glad you're here." He exhaled, as if he'd been holding his breath, not sure she'd come. "There's a lot of interest in your donation."

"I'm shocked. Your description of my service must be the hook. Thanks for making it sound so good."

She moved away from the auction table, and Dean followed.

"Is something on your mind?" he asked. He was most definitely tuned in to her.

She cleared her throat. "I've had an interesting week." And confusing. Perhaps he could weigh in. "One of the owners of a company I delivered cookies to had seen the videos my mom and I posted, so he knew I was a lawyer. He started asking questions about the transformation of my parents' business. By the end of the conversation, he wanted to know if I could study his business and come up with a plan to restructure and market it."

Dean's lips twitched, holding back a smile. "That's great. What did you say?"

"I told him I was returning to New York as soon as I found a job." She paused, not wanting to ruin their night but also needing to be honest. "I got a call today from my headhunter. He has an offer for me."

His smile disappeared. "I assume it's in New York?"

She nodded.

"Are you taking it?" Disappointment shadowed his jade gaze, and his face paled.

"I told him I'd get back to him on Monday." She hoped to hear him say something that would encourage her to think twice about the offer, but his silence was deafening. "I'll probably take it. I have no other offers, and this is a good one."

"Is it the same type of work you were doing?"

She winced, a hard ball forming in her stomach. "Yes."

"You said you didn't like the work. That you were going to consider other options."

"I have no other options, and I need a job. I can't let too much time pass, or I'll be less marketable." The stress of her plight moved from her stomach to her chest, squeezing her lungs.

"Do you see all those bids on that sheet for your custom business proposal? Every single one of those people want you to help them. And while only the highest bidder will win that privilege, my guess is that the rest of them would be willing to pay you whatever you charge to do the same for them. I know most of those bidders, and they could all use help in taking their business to the next level."

"Are you suggesting that I start my own business

here?" An overwhelming proposal.

"Why not try something new? You're young. You're smart. You're savvy. And if I'm not mistaken, you've loved every minute of planning and executing your ideas for your parents' business."

He was right. She was loving it. Although she would have loved it more if they hadn't had to do it in so little time.

She looked at him, astonished that he had seen all that. "You are very perceptive."

"Does that mean you'll give it a go?"

"It means I'll think about it." While she had jumped in with both feet to help her parents, when it came to her next move, she needed to consider all the pros and cons.

But her insides smiled. Dean had weighed in as she'd hoped, not only to dissuade her from taking a job she knew she'd loathe, but to propose a plan to start her own business. Here. Then he upped the ante.

"Just your thinking about it calls for a celebration."

He took two glasses of champagne from a roving waiter and handed one to her. His penetrating gaze held her captive, and the temperature in the room rose as her blood raced through her veins.

"If there's anything I can do to persuade you to stay—"

His beautiful lips parted, as if an invitation to a kiss, and she floated in his aura. Long fingers glided to her cheek, his touch intoxicating. The din of the crowd surrounding them disappeared, and all she saw, all she heard, was him.

"I don't want you to leave, Bella."

Words—too inadequate to explain the emotions churning through her—clogged her throat and tied her tongue. She couldn't speak.

A shadow dimmed his eyes, recasting them from emerald to celadon. Was it disappointment in her lack of response?

He clinked her glass with his. "To the future."

Chapter Eleven

Bella packed the trunk of her mom's car with the last of the orders on her delivery schedule, double-checking her list.

"Hi, Bella."

Dean's warm voice branded her heart despite the mere words of greeting. "Hey, Dean."

"Still in work mode even though it's Christmas Eve? What time are you finished?"

Her gaze wandered over his broad chest and up to his smiling face. "I should have my deliveries done by three. My parents are closing the shop at four."

"Good. Come to my house for dinner tonight at six."

It wasn't a question. He must be through asking politely, only to hear excuse after excuse. Yes, she had been busy. But she had also been grappling with her career decision while at the same time shielding her heart. He'd said he wanted her to stay on Saturday night. And the sizzling electricity between them couldn't be imaginary. But could she rearrange her whole life—the life she'd worked so hard to achieve in the big city—over the possibility of a relationship with Dean? Deep down, she knew this decision had to be made because she wanted to make this change for herself.

"I…I think my parents are expecting me to have dinner with them tonight."

"I already checked with them. They're fine if you

have other plans."

Smart man. Getting her parents on board with his plot. Although, really, they'd been fans of his for years.

She sighed, but her smile escaped. "Of course they are."

****

She arrived at his house a few minutes after six. She had dressed for the occasion, shunning her usual jeans and sweater for an emerald-green, silk dress and sparkly, strappy heels. Armed with a gift box of cookies as well as a small token for her dinner host—she rang the doorbell.

Dean opened the door, a designer suit cleaving to his broad shoulders and lean muscles.

She swallowed her desire and went for admiration. "You certainly look good in tailored suits."

He took her hand and pulled her into the foyer before slipping off her coat. He arched a brow as his gaze roamed over her curves. "Beautiful. I thought red was your color the other night. But emerald looks just as good."

The color reminded her of his eyes, but she kept that to herself, taking in the Christmas decorations exploding before her. Huge nutcrackers lined the entrance hall with boughs of greenery and gold ribbon festooning the circular stair railing. A great room took up the entire left side of the house with an open-beamed ceiling perfect for his ten-foot Christmas tree decorated with hundreds of colorful ornaments and lights.

"Wow. You must love Christmas." An electric train ran around the base of the tree with a village painstakingly set out in its quaint glory. "Did you do all this yourself?"

He laughed, and it rumbled around her insides.

"Of course. I bought a lot of the ornaments over the years from your parents' shop. Your mom's big on nutcrackers."

"It looks wonderful." She handed him the box of cookies as well as the wrapped gift.

He took both offerings and laid the cookie box on the mahogany entrance table. "I hope this contains red velvet crinkles."

"Of course. I know your weakness."

"Come on in." He ushered her to the sofa, taking the gift-wrapped box with him. "Can I open this now?"

"Please do."

A bottle of champagne sat in an ice bucket, and two flutes waited nearby. A cutting board held a variety of cheeses, and a Christmas plate was filled with crackers. What would he have done with all this if she'd cancelled at the last minute in a fit of panic?

He unwrapped his gift and removed the delicate tree ornament from its nest of tissue paper before holding it up to the light. "This is beautiful. It reminds me of the gingerbread houses at Cobblestone Village."

"That's what I was going for. A happy memory, I hope."

It was more than that to her. Dean had kissed her that day. Her entire high school career, she'd dreamed of that. Unrequited love left an ache in her heart that even in later years hadn't entirely disappeared.

"The best memory."

He walked over to the tree, somehow found an unadorned limb, and hung the new ornament in a place of honor. Then he bent down and took a wrapped box from under the tree. "Merry Christmas." He sat down beside her and handed her his gift.

"You weren't supposed to get me anything." Her fingers shook as she unwrapped the present, finding a dainty gold necklace with an engraved message. *Some women fear the fire. Some simply become it.*

She looked up at him, exhilaration surging at his belief in her. "This is beautiful. I love the quote. Thank you."

"You are one of the strongest women I know. I've watched you over the past few weeks take a failing business, jump in with both feet, and turn it around. You are fire, Bella."

Tears flooded her eyes, and words caught in her throat. "I'm not sure that it's completely turned around yet."

"It's heading in the right direction. Can I put this on for you?" He took the necklace from her hand.

She nodded, then swiveled so her back was to him and held up her hair.

He slid the chain around her neck, and his fingers caused a riot as they skimmed her nape, his warm breath sending flames to her core.

She turned back to face him, raising her fingers to caress the pendant that held the empowering words. "This means a lot to me."

He sobered. "You mean a lot to me." His warm palm caressed her cheek. "I'm falling in love with you, Bella."

Time stopped, and rampaging sensations robbed her of breath. Joy bubbled up inside and spilled out. "I've been falling in love with you since high school."

Swirling emotions cocooned her, and she tilted her head up and met his lips for a fiercely tender kiss.

He pulled back but cradled her face as his eyes

connected with her soul. "Will you stay in Princeton?"

All reservations disappeared in a flash. She had prized creating a business and marketing plan for her parents' dwindling sales. She had cherished making connections with the local business owners in the spirit of community. And she had loved getting to know the real Dean, the man who was devoted to his family's business as well as to her parents, who was kind enough to help her help them despite her surly attitude toward him. The man who didn't give up on her in the face of all her rejections, denials, and snubs.

"The pros far outweigh the cons," she rasped. "I believe I can say with one hundred percent commitment that I'm ready to embrace a new life, a new career, and open my own business here in Princeton."

His smile dazzled like a million twinkly lights. "That's the best Christmas gift I could ever receive."

Tinsel and Tea Cakes

by

Jill Piscitello

Christmas Cookies Series

Dedication

For Rob, Kaelie, and Anthony

Chapter One

With the change in altitude, Scarlett's ears grew more plugged by the minute as her ruby red sedan climbed what were supposed to be the picturesque White Mountains in New Hampshire. The headlights strained to cut through the blinding snow, but she couldn't see two feet ahead on the slick road and prayed the car had at least entered Hemlock Bend by now.

Aching fingers gripped the steering wheel with increasing intensity as she berated herself. What in the world had made her agree to navigate through a snowstorm en route to a wedding for a bride and groom she'd never met? If anyone other than her stepmother asked, she would have flatly refused to attend. She stole a glance at Clarice, asleep in the passenger seat. At least one of them was enjoying a peaceful ride.

This shindig better be worth it. Nearly everyone in New England had heard about the elaborate occasions hosted by The Timeless Manor. They took party themes to a whole new level. A lavish medieval wedding? Done. A 1970s, disco-infused anniversary party? Easy. If a client named it, the staff planned it, leaving no detail omitted. The venue even housed a warehouse full of rental period costumes to coincide with their most popular themes. To Scarlett, it sounded like they ran elaborate dress-up parties.

Clarice wouldn't know a soul at this weekend's

Victorian Christmas nuptials other than the mother of the bride and a few co-workers. But she wasn't about to miss this wedding for the world and prodded and poked at Scarlett until she'd finally given in and agreed to attend as her plus one. She'd never be hurtful enough to point out Scarlett had nothing else to do, even if it was the cold, hard truth. The salon where she'd worked for seven years closed, and the commitment-phobe she'd dated for the last five months announced his engagement to the woman long decreed to be nothing more than a good friend. These two events culminated with Scarlett's penniless, rejected self moving into Clarice's over fifty-five condo complex. Who was she to pass up an all-expenses paid trip to the mountains for a three-day weekend?

Thoughts of mooning around Clarice's place all weekend didn't belong on this trip. Relentless, dizzying flakes flew toward the windshield, demanding her undivided attention. The car lurched to the right without warning on tires assuming a mind of their own, and faded images of sweatpants and ice cream evaporated. An unfamiliar guttural sound escaped her lips, but muscle memory kicked in, thanks to years of winter driving. Without breathing, she eased her foot off the brake and steered into the skid.

"What is going on?" Clarice blinked awake and braced a hand on the dashboard.

A pulsing heartbeat thundered in her ears, drowning out the urge to remind her dear stepmother that dashboards don't provide better protection than seatbelts. She put the car in Park, exhaled a whoosh of air, and tucked shaking hands under her thighs to still them. Despite her rattled nerves, a giggle bubbled up. "I think my life might have flashed before my eyes. I'm embarrassed to say it was a rather dull reel."

With a huff, Clarice re-adjusted herself. "Well, this isn't the excitement I was hoping for. Let's get on with it." A flick of the wrist jangled a cluster of bracelets. "We can't sit here all day."

A litany of barbed comments threatened to spew forth, but Scarlett swallowed every last one, shifted into Drive, and stepped on the gas. The wheels spun in place, and a wave of nausea washed over her. She never should have agreed to this trip.

Lights flashed in the side view mirror. Another car parked behind them, but snow blocked all visibility through the back window. Boots crunching through snow announced the hulking figure before he appeared at the door. A scarf and hat covered most of the stranger's face, and only a pair of emerald-green eyes peered in.

Scarlett inched down the window a crack. The possibility of this person being a deranged lunatic couldn't be overlooked.

"Scarlett?" The man stepped back and tugged down the scarf.

She knew that face and opened her mouth to speak but couldn't find a word. This day just kept getting better. Those eyes should have been the first clue, but never in her wildest dreams did she expect to see him again. The blur of memories racing through her mind dropped a throat-constricting concoction of confusion, hurt, and vile hope on her chest. "Wes."

"What are you doing here? Aren't you a little far from home?" A line formed between his eyebrows.

Clarice leaned forward to get a better glimpse of

their potential knight in shining armor.

"More than a little." Coherent thoughts took shape in the form of questions and accusations. Every fiber in her being burned at the thought of asking him for help, but alternative options were few and far between. Who knew how long before roadside assistance arrived? Fine, maybe he'd get her out of this mess, but making small talk didn't need to factor into the exchange. "Any chance you have a shovel? If we can dig out my wheels a bit, I might have a chance of moving."

"Give me a minute." He trudged over to his car.

The heat from Clarice's gaze bore into the back of her head and slid down her neck.

"How do you know him?"

A telltale lilt crept into Clarice's voice. Scarlett released a breath and met her inquisitive gaze. "We crossed paths a while back. I don't know him well." At least not as well as she'd once thought.

"Let's hope this works." Clarice sat back and held up her phone. "I'm not getting a signal, and you probably aren't either."

"He's coming back." Scarlett pulled on a hat and gloves. She opened the door and stepped into the frigid air.

"Get back in the car. This isn't a two-person job— at least until I get some of this cleared away." Without waiting for a response, he plunged the shovel into the snow.

Scarlett snapped her mouth closed. Who did he think she was, a helpless damsel in distress, incapable of using a shovel? On second thought, let him have at it. This wasn't the time to wave her independent woman flag in his face. A bit of manual labor was the least he could do after what he'd put her through. Ducking her head did little to stave off the wind whipping wet flakes into her eyes. As she climbed inside, the animated expression on Clarice's face shredded any lingering threads of patience.

"Where'd you meet? You know, a chance encounter such as this might just be the kick in the pants you need to stop moping around over that good-for-nothin' Niall."

Great. Another lecture on the time she'd wasted with Niall Olsen and an interrogation asking how she knew Wes Harley. Sure, Clarice meant well. But they'd reached the tail end of a four-hour, treacherous drive from Rhode Island. Getting out of this car and off the road couldn't happen fast enough.

"Right now, I'm focused on reaching our destination in one piece. In case you haven't noticed, we're driving through a freakin' blizzard." A flicker of guilt settled on her chest. Getting snappy with Clarice wouldn't help matters. Desperate for a diversion from all subjects, Scarlett twisted the dial on the radio, found a cheery Christmas station, and cranked up the volume to drown out the sounds of the shovel crunching through snow and any further questions. With her stomach clenched into a tight ball, she rested her head against the seat and closed her eyes against the flakes piling up.

A dull thud propelled her forward. Newly accumulated snow disappeared from her windshield and revealed Wes, now an abominable snowman. Her resolve to maintain a steely vibe softened. Watching him approach the window, she fought the half smile tugging at the corners of her mouth.

"I think you're all set. When you hear me knock on your trunk, put the car in Drive, and I'll push. Once you're on the road, just keep going."

"Thanks, Wes." Unable to meet his penetrating stare, she averted her gaze. Did he have something else to say? Well, he could save it. Any heartfelt apologies should have been offered a year ago. Or worse, was he waiting for her to say more? She wasn't about to grovel in gratitude.

"Where are you headed?" he asked. "I hope it's not far."

That made two of them. Abandoning her car on the side of the road and asking for a lift was tempting. But the more rational side of her brain took over, admonishing that Wes Harley was not someone to depend on. "Once we get going, we'll be fine."

"Well, drive safely."

Maintaining a solid break in eye contact was her best bet for putting an end to this chance encounter. She couldn't help herself and darted her gaze toward him for a microsecond. Was that sincere concern etching his forehead? "You, too." She closed the window and shifted the car into Drive.

His frame, bulkier than she remembered due to the parka, continued to block the light of the deep gray sky. If he took the hint and left, they both could pretend this encounter never happened. The beginning of an endless loop of reasons for his continued presence ignited a furious gallop in her chest. As he backed away, light poured into her window. She willed herself to stare straight ahead and steered the sedan onto the road.

Although flooded with relief to be moving, she spent the remainder of the drive wondering for the umpteenth time what happened last year. He'd allowed her to believe they had a future and then cut off all contact. One text message with a whopping seven words sealed the deal.

—I'm sorry. This isn't going to work.—

Her subsequent calls and texts were ignored. Maybe she'd given up too easily, but she refused to chase after anyone. She'd never been "that girl."

Despite a few wrong turns due to a spotty signal, Scarlett didn't need a phone to announce their arrival. Towering stone pillars appeared on either side of a private road. A whitewashed brick chateau loomed ahead at the end of the lengthy, circular driveway lined with snow-cloaked trees.

Staff dressed in full-length black coats assisted guests exiting their cars and relinquishing their keys.

She idled behind four other cars and gaped at the sight before them.

"We've literally stepped back in time," whispered Clarice.

"Good thing the storm is letting up. Can you imagine these poor people having to put on this show a half hour ago?" Several minutes passed before she drove all the way up to the house.

A stout man with a ramrod-straight posture and beet-red cheeks tapped the driver window. His dark coat and pants prevented the starched white of his shirt and bow tie from blending into the scenery.

"Shut off the car and unlock the doors," said Clarice.

Two footmen approached.

Clarice fumbled to unbuckle her seat belt before the door swung open.

"Good day, milady! Welcome to The Timeless Manor. I'm Edward. If you'd kindly pass me your keys, we'll handle your luggage, and Lucy will show you to your rooms."

"Uh, th-thank you." Scarlett wondered if his impeccable English accent was authentic. As she stepped out and handed over the keys, an arctic blast of cold air tore into her bones.

Lucy rushed toward them, her unbuttoned coat flapping open to reveal a formal maid's costume circa late 1800s complete with a white apron over a plain, black dress, black tights, and a square of lace resembling a white doily pinned on top of her head.

Wincing, Scarlett bit back the urge to suggest the woman button up and find some footwear more appropriate to the weather.

"Welcome." Through chattering teeth, Lucy smiled. "Your name, please."

"Scarlett Kerrigan. I'm here with Clarice Brady." She gestured toward the opposite side of the car.

"Wonderful. Follow me, and we'll get you both settled in." Lucy motioned to a lanky bellhop laden with their bags. She spun on her heel and marched them along the cleared, brick herringbone walkway, up the steps, and into the house.

A blast of warmth and a gleaming white Christmas tree towering to the top of the ceiling greeted guests in the foyer where Scarlett stomped snow from her boots onto the doormat. As she followed Lucy past the tree and around a corner, mingling scents of spruce, cinnamon, and freshly baked cookies beckoned.

A woman sat behind a large, ornate desk ringed in silver garland adorned with miniature pink and purple ornaments.

The receptionist's iced pink pixie failed to achieve Victorian era hairstyle expectations but coordinated with the decorations and added a touch of whimsy. Heat radiated across the room from the blazing fireplace surrounded by several guests already settled in.

"Lady Kerrigan and Lady Brady are joining us this afternoon," announced Lucy.

Lady? Scarlett stifled a laugh.

Clarice's fingertips flew to her lips, concealing a grin.

"Wonderful," the woman replied. She rifled around in a drawer and produced two key cards. "Lady Scarlett, you'll be staying in the Silver Room. Lady Clarice, you're right next door in the Lavender Room. My name is Betty. If you need anything at all, dial star-seven-seven using your room telephone, and I or another staff member will be happy to help."

"This way please." Lucy led them to the top of the sweeping, holly-trimmed staircase and pointed down the hallway of doors decorated with wreaths and red velvet ribbons. Each displayed a placard with room names scrawled in calligraphy. "Your rooms are ahead on the left. I expect you'll both be quite comfortable."

Scarlett swiped her card and opened the door.

The tune of Clarice sucking in her breath pierced the pristine space.

Silver Room indeed. The queen bed included a silver, cushioned headboard and a plush, white comforter edged in satiny silver and plump white pillows. A white settee sat at the foot of the bed with a lush, oversized white throw trimmed in silver pom poms. The light switched on, and Scarlett tipped her neck back to gaze at the delicate, crystal chandelier centered on the ceiling. But the true focal point of the room demanded her undivided attention.

Wide, sheer ribbon, white poinsettias, tiny lights, and a few strategically placed shimmering silver ornaments enhanced the already lovely, snow-tipped faux tree beside a picture window overlooking the grounds. Scarlett followed her nose to the table on the other side of the window and grinned at the plate of cookies, coffee machine, and hot chocolate packet stuffed into a mug, calling her name. Her stomach rumbled, reminding her she'd passed famished hours ago.

"Oh, that does it. If your room looks like this, I'm not waiting one minute more to see mine. And there better be cookies."

The bellhop stepped forward. "Pardon me, ma'am."

"Milady," whispered Lucy.

Scarlett smiled to herself and turned. She wouldn't argue with that logic. "Milady" sounded far more charming than ma'am.

"The blue bags are mine." She dug into her purse to find a tip.

Gangly arms dropped two totes on the floor and reshuffled the remaining, overloaded pieces of luggage. With beads of sweat breaking out on his forehead, the young man accepted the money and bumped his way through the doorjamb.

Squeals rang out from the next room. She tossed her purse onto the bed and dashed into the hallway.

Lucy and the bellhop stood at the open door. Both held a hand to their mouth but failed to hide their laughter.

Clarice zipped about fawning over every detail. She spotted Scarlett entering and sagged down on buckling knees. "Can you believe this place?" She threw out her arms and twirled.

"I cannot." Laughing, Scarlett leaned against the dresser. The room dripped in Christmas decorations, but with a lavender color scheme. "You and I can spend the rest of the afternoon in disbelief, but we need to let these two attend to other guests."

"Absolutely." She fluttered over to the bed, drew some bills from her purse, and waved them toward the amused staff.

"Larson did all the heavy lifting." Lucy motioned toward the bellhop and stepped into the hall. "Please let us know if you need anything. Dinner is served at six thirty, but a light lunch is available in the sunroom now."

Scarlett closed the door and spun to face her stepmother. "This place is really something."

Engulfed in the luxurious throw she'd draped over her shoulders, Clarice plopped down on the edge of the bed and flashed a grin. "Can I say I told you so?"

"Nothing's ever stopped you before. At least this time, you earned that triumphant glow." She glanced at her watch. "Let's freshen up, see what lunch looks like, and then explore."

"Sounds like a plan." Clarice hopped up and shrugged off the blanket. "Give me fifteen minutes."

Scarlett froze.

"That face! What's wrong?"

She jammed a hand into each back pocket of her jeans and found both empty. "My key card!" Groaning, she sank into a nearby chair. "I heard all the commotion in here and locked myself out of my room."

"Star-seven-seven!" Clarice pranced over to the telephone on her nightstand and commiserated with the front desk about the hilarity of the situation. Still chuckling, she replaced the receiver and excused herself to change into something more flattering than wrinkled traveling clothes.

At the first rap on the door, Scarlett shot to her feet and yanked it open. Her stomach flipped over. The expression passing over the man's chiseled face matched her own state of shock.

Chapter Two

Scarlett swallowed hard and staggered back. "Wes."
A flickering image of closing Clarice's door in his face
flashed through her mind. "What are you doing here?"

His gaze soared to the ceiling. "Where have I heard
those words before?"

"I'm serious." She folded her arms across her chest
and jutted out her chin. "Did you follow me?"

He smirked. "I work here. The guest staying in this
room reported her neighbor being locked out."

Heat flamed her cheeks. Why hadn't she taken off
her coat before rushing over? A blazing inferno coursed
through her veins, and perspiration threatened to erupt
on her forehead. A freak coincidence was one thing. But
two? "You work here?"

He jangled a set of plastic cards on a metal ring.

"I…okay. I left my key card inside my room."

"Not a problem."

His casual stride down the hall implying nothing at
all was odd about this situation singed already frayed
nerves.

With one swipe, he unlocked the door.

"Thank you." Why wasn't he moving? She clenched
her teeth and brushed past him. Familiar notes of
sandalwood hung in the air, evoking memories she
thought had been put to rest.

"You must be here for the wedding."

"Yeah." She shook her head but failed to comprehend the idea of running into him twice today. "I'm sorry. I just didn't expect to see you. Again."

He shifted from one foot to the other and averted his gaze.

Good. He deserved to feel uncomfortable, even if he did come to their rescue earlier.

"Wes?" rang out a voice from the end of the hall.

A woman with a sleek, platinum bob wearing a tailored navy suit strode down the hallway.

"When you're finished here, I need you to stop by the kitchen and make sure we're on schedule for tonight." She stopped and extended a hand toward Scarlett. "Hello, I'm Vivian. Welcome to The Timeless Manor."

"Thank you." The birdlike woman's hand gripped her own with surprising strength. "My stepmother and I are excited to be here. The staff's attention to detail has already surpassed expectations." She scrunched up her nose. "If I possessed a fraction of their efficiency, I wouldn't be standing out here."

"Is everything okay?" Two lines formed between Vivian's eyebrows.

"Oh, yes." The lie slid easily from her lips. "I accidentally locked myself out of my room. Wes just let me back in."

Vivian raised a hand to her heart, and her face relaxed into a smile. All signs of expression lines disappeared. "Happens to the best of us. Did you have a long drive?"

"A little more than four hours."

"You must be half starved." The woman gripped Wes's elbow. "Make sure she finds a decent lunch downstairs."

"Will do, Mother." His gaze veered toward the top of the stairs.

A girl, maybe six or seven years old, bounded toward them waving a cell phone above her head. Blonde curls flew in every direction.

"Dad." She thrust the phone at Wes. "Mommy wants to talk to you."

In slow motion, Scarlett swayed and placed a hand on the doorjamb. The ringing in her ears drowned out their voices. She strained to process the few words that broke through. *Dad? Mommy?*

Vivian smiled. "I would love to stay and chat, but duty calls." She clasped the child's hand. "Come with me, Maisie. I'm putting you to work in the kitchen taste testing tonight's desserts."

Fixated on the child whose hair of spun gold and captivating eyes matched that of the man standing before her, Scarlett straightened. A searing surge of anger replaced previous states of shock and confusion. Speechless, she turned her head and studied his unreadable expression.

Wes frowned at the phone.

Who was the woman waiting on the other end of the line? His wife? A girlfriend? He wouldn't dare answer it with her standing right here. Too bad. She wasn't going anywhere.

Humming a Christmas carol, Clarice emerged from her room.

A cloud of jasmine wafted into the hallway. Her arrival interrupted a conversation Scarlett didn't know how, and didn't want, to begin.

"Ready, dear?"

"Uh, not yet." She searched Clarice's face for any sign of recognition and found none. She must not have gotten a good enough look at Wes on the road.

"Excuse me. Would you happen to know what time lunch is over?" Clarice asked a now-rigid Wes.

His head jerked up. "In about an hour. You have time."

Unable to suffer that deceitful face for another second, Scarlett whirled around and entered her room on jelly legs.

Before the door closed, Clarice scooted in. "You didn't waste any time, did you?"

Not again. That signature childlike chirping she used every time she put on her matchmaker hat. "That was nothing more than an employee assisting a guest."

Clarice raised an eyebrow. "Sure. The tension between you two nearly choked me. Now go get yourself prettified before I pass out from sheer starvation."

An excuse to escape another uninvited romantic consultation? Please, and thank you. Scarlett made a beeline for the bathroom. She gripped the edge of the sink with both hands and stared at her stricken reflection. How could she be so stupid? Of course, he was married. Of course, he had a child. Of course, he'd wanted nothing to do with her after a chance meeting in Aruba. Right now, vomiting the bile from her empty stomach was more appealing than joining Clarice for lunch.

How was she supposed to survive a weekend brimming with Clarice's well-intended ploys to help her get over the just-been-dumped blues while crossing paths with Wes time and time again? Clarice possessed a perspective alien to Scarlett. The woman didn't have the faintest idea how serving as a mere placeholder in a man's life felt, while he waited for "the one" to arrive or as a flirty way to pass the hours away from his wife. The time had come for Scarlett to take a step back and learn how to size up men with a more discerning eye before diving in headfirst. She'd made that mistake too many times in the past.

Hopping from one dead-end relationship to another benefited no one. She craved a break from the endless search for Mr. Perfect. He might very well exist, but she'd never find him by settling for romances of convenience. What did she want, and what did she need? Both answers would play a role. Her serial dating days were over.

****

Unable to focus on the voice chattering away on the other end of the line, Wes stared at the closed door. Adrienne rambled at her mile-a-minute pace about the gifts she'd shipped to Maisie.

"Now, you need to make sure a total of seventeen packages arrived. They should all be there by now."

"I'll be sure to count them and send you a text confirming everything made it." He disconnected the call before she could throw more instructions. Should he knock on Scarlett's door? She hadn't given him a chance to explain. Not that he blamed her. The thoughts that must be running through her head right now…

The phone buzzed in his hand with a new text message. What possible emergency occurred in the on-site salon? Whatever Scarlett was or was not thinking must wait. In fact, he welcomed the interruption. She had a guest in her room, and the last thing he wanted was an audience for what would be a difficult conversation.

As he approached the salon, raised voices carried

through the closed, French doors. His mother, Lucy, and Edward, engaged in a heated discussion, didn't notice him enter. "What's going on?" he shouted over them.

For the briefest moment, a welcome silence replaced the commotion.

"I don't know where to begin," his mother snapped. A thin vein bulged in the middle of her forehead.

Lucy took a deep breath and stepped forward. "It's Skylar. She slipped on some stairs this morning and broke her ankle. We had to cancel her run-through appointment with the bride for this afternoon, and she can't make it here tomorrow morning."

"We don't have a hairdresser?" He inhaled, forced his tense shoulders to relax, and silently reassured himself. Every wedding comes with minor snags. Maintaining one's composure is the key to creative solutions.

"The bride is livid," Lucy said. "She had some updo styles she hoped to try out ahead of time, and now we don't even know if we can find another stylist for tomorrow."

"Mom, can't you make some calls and find someone to fill in?"

Vivian fidgeted with her diamond pendant and frowned. "I've called everyone I could think of. Between Christmas and the snow, we're out of luck."

Myra White had inhabited this salon for over two decades. She'd retired two years ago, and they'd yet to find a suitable replacement. He'd scheduled Skylar for her first full weekend at the manor. If things went well, he was prepared to offer her the opportunity to rent the chair full time. So much for that grand idea.

The Timeless Manor boasted a long-held,

outstanding reputation as an event venue. But this weekend's wedding was of particular importance. A review from the McKay and Donovan families could make or break future business.

Scarlett. What were the chances she'd be willing to help out? Slim to none, but zero if he didn't ask. "I need to check on something. I'll catch up with you guys in a few."

One fringe benefit of employing long-term staff was relying on a work family of seasoned experts at defusing the look of horror distorting his mother's features. He left without a backward glance. Scarlett might be his only hope of salvaging this disastrous wedding. But before falling in supplication at her feet, he owed her an apology and an explanation. Would it be enough?

****

Scarlett paused at the entrance to the sunroom and let the tantalizing aromas of today's luncheon wash over her. She deserved a pat on the back for refusing to allow the likes of Wes Harley to ruin her good time. This spread of all things delicious was her reward. Buffet tables set up in each corner of the room beckoned.

With a hand pressed to her chest, Clarice whistled and arched back.

"Pace yourself, Clarice," Scarlett chided. "You'll want to save room for dinner."

"Sage advice."

The voice from behind set off a fresh batch of heart palpitations in Scarlett's chest.

Clarice winked at Wes. "You distract her while I get the lay of the land." She hustled to the nearest carving station.

"Is that your mom?" Wes asked.

She scanned the room. The architect who designed this place must have decided the inclusion of an unobtrusive escape route required too much effort. Resigned to the fact she had nowhere to run, she returned his stare. "Stepmom. Clarice was my dad's partner for twenty-three years."

His gaze flicked over her shoulder. "Let's get you a table so she has somewhere to put down her plates."

"Plates?" She swung around.

Leave it to Clarice to balance two full-size dinner plates and a small salad while still scoping out the goods. The woman was a bottomless pit. The way she ate, they'd need a table for four.

Scarlett gave in and, dodging a group of swaying guests clearly not on their first round of mimosas, followed Wes to one of the tables lining a row of windows providing a glorious view of the mountains and the last whispers of falling snow. "Thank you." She dragged out a white, ladder-back chair and sat.

"Aren't you getting something to eat?" He leaned forward with both hands on the back of the chair opposite her.

"Yeah. But when Clarice joins me, she'll be in near distress over not fitting something on her plate, correction—plates, that caught her eye. I'll wait and pick up the order when I hit the buffets for myself."

"Where does she put it?"

"Your guess is as good as mine."

Clarice pranced over and deposited her dishes on the table with a thud. "You two stay put so the waitstaff doesn't come along and snatch my goodies. I still need to find a cup of coffee."

"Daphne can take care of beverages." Wes flagged

over a server. "Other than helping yourself to the buffet tables, you don't need to lift a finger."

A young woman wearing a maid's uniform hurried over with a full pot of coffee and flipped over two of the four mugs on the table.

"Join us for a bit." Clarice patted the seat next to her. "Perhaps you can teach me how to sound a bit more British, so I can fully immerse myself in the Victorian experience."

"Clarice, I'm sure he's busy." Scarlett could do without a small talk session with a two-timing liar.

Instead of leaving, Wes smirked and accepted the seat. "I am. Starting with keeping your delightful companion company while you get your food."

Overruled, Scarlett glanced from one to the other and stood, deciding on the best course of action to rid him from their table. But the beaming, pleased-as-punch smile on Clarice's face spelled failure. Her stepmother wasn't about to let this one go without a fight. "If you're sure? I'll only be a minute or two."

"Take your time." Wes shifted his gaze toward Clarice and cupped a hand near his mouth. "I see you went with the lemon squares. Legend has it these particular squares are enchanted."

"Oh, I can't wait to hear why." She picked up one with her fingertips and inspected each corner.

Dismissed, Scarlett strolled the perimeter of the room, checked out all the manor offered, and then headed for the turkey-carving station. But the line, seven people deep, didn't appear to be moving. Was the wait worth risking the other food growing cold?

She popped a scallop wrapped in bacon in her mouth and suppressed a moan. Hot or lukewarm, these pickings fell nothing short of perfection. At the very least, this line would provide a few extra minutes to find a gracious way to send Wes on his way. Maybe she assumed too much. If he possessed any social graces, he'd already have an acceptable excuse ready to go before she returned.

A screech pealed at a nearby table.

Every gaze in the room fell on a woman shoving aside plates and tossing napkins.

She dropped to the floor, crawled under the table, and emerged seconds later from the other side with her hair in disarray. "My bracelet!" she shrieked. "It's gone!" She blew bangs out of her eyes and tried in vain to smooth her staticky head. The woman scrambled to her feet, lunged toward the nearest buffet, and used bare hands to dig through platters of food.

Everyone watched wide-eyed in silence.

Wes approached and rested a palm against his chest. "Mrs. McKay, I understand your frustration. Let's just catch a breath for a minute."

"Catch your own breath!" she snapped. "Do you have any idea what that bracelet is worth?"

"I'm confident we'll find it. We'll search this room and then retrace your steps."

The reassurance in his voice amidst the watchful gaze of a rapt audience did little to appease the woman. Scarlett fought the urge to intervene. Adding her two cents might worsen the situation.

"No one is leaving until it's found. Your staff and guests can consider themselves in lockdown."

"Mrs. McKay, several people have come and gone in the last hour. I firmly believe if someone finds the bracelet, they will return it to the front desk."

The woman stalked back to her table and made a

failed attempt to wipe her hands clean. She threw down the napkin and yanked a cardigan from the back of a chair. "You give people too much credit. I'm finding Vivian, and I might be filing a police report."

Wes exhaled and stared at the silent guests. "I'm sorry about this…this unfortunate event. Please resume an enjoyable meal and trust we will work to resolve the issue as soon as possible."

Transfixed, Scarlett hadn't moved from the line. Across the room, Clarice still hadn't remembered to close her mouth. What's a wedding without a touch of drama?

Chapter Three

For someone who thought she'd lost her appetite, Scarlett demolished everything on her plate. She sat back with a contented sigh. The food was to die for. The cup of clam chowder, slab of fried cod, turkey, and two lemon squares were worth their weight in calories. But if she continued to indulge in the manor's delicacies, would her dress refuse to zip tomorrow? A more sensible choice might be something with an empire waist, but Scarlett had ordered a late 1800s ball gown complete with a corset. At this rate, the waist cinching torture device would likely remain on the hanger.

Clarice popped the last bite of lemon square into her mouth and closed her eyes.

Unaware of a gentleman with white hair and a white beard approaching the table, her expression implied a true state of bliss.

"Enjoying the food, I hope." The man's gaze flitted between them.

If he wasn't so thin, he might have passed for Santa Claus. "Outstanding," Scarlett replied.

Swallowing, Clarice opened her eyes. "I'll say. That piece of heaven tasted like another. I sampled nearly everything on display, and I'm already getting excited to see what the dinner menu entails."

A small uproar erupted at the entrance to the sunroom. Scarlett swiveled in her seat and sucked in a sharp breath. The most striking woman she'd ever seen stood preening before a gaggle of admirers.

Jet-black hair skimmed bronzed shoulders and framed a dewy, heavily made-up face. The woman wore a strapless, red jumpsuit cinched at the waist with a string of crystals. Teetering above a pair of crystal embellished, strappy stilettos, she blew kisses and princess waves to the guests.

"That's quite a lunch outfit," Clarice whispered across the table.

Unfortunately, whispering wasn't her strength. Scarlett tapped a foot under the table until she found her target and lobbed a light kick at her stepmother's shoe.

The man still standing nearby laughed out loud. "Should I assume you have yet to be introduced to the bride?"

"That's the bride?" Scarlett asked. "Too bad she can't bottle that brand of confidence for the rest of us."

"Very true. When Harper enters a room, she makes sure everyone knows it." He fixed his attention on them and stretched out a hand toward Clarice. "I'm forgetting my manners. I'm the bride's great uncle, Graham, and am well acquainted with the spectacle of Harper McKay."

After flipping her hair to one side, Clarice accepted his hand. "I'm Clarice, and this is Scarlett. I work for Millie, the bride's mother."

"Ah, Millie's my niece. Her mother is my sister." Still holding her hand, he leaned forward. "We should have a cup of coffee, and I'll tell you all the company secrets. I worked at the McKay's marketing firm for thirty-three years. Most members of our family end up in the family business at one point or another."

Clarice twitched her shoulders and tilted her chin downward while glancing up through doe-like lashes. "I'm not one to gossip, but I do love a good cup of coffee."

They were flirting! Straightening her spine, Scarlett sat back against her seat. Only Clarice would traipse all over town for the last two years demanding her senior discount, yet still wrap a smitten man around her manicured finger. Years ago, Scarlett learned to balance missing her father without begrudging Clarice the opportunity to have a bit of fun. But the little dance playing out rattled her tentative grip on composure. "Please, take my seat." She stood. "I'm in desperate need of a few minutes alone to unpack and freshen up."

"It would be my pleasure." With a wink, Graham released his grip on Clarice and sat.

I have no doubt. Scarlett slung her purse over her shoulder and pecked Clarice on the cheek. "Text me later." She stifled a giggle. Not even a halfhearted insistence to join them was offered. As she ascended the grand staircase, a smattering of odd notes from the band arranging instruments in the foyer jangled. Maybe by the time she returned, they'd be playing.

The door clicked shut, and the most satisfying silence enveloped her. Scarlett flopped onto the bed and lay back with eyes closed, savoring the solitude for several exquisite minutes. Not one thirty yet, and every muscle in her body insisted a full day had passed. She would love, love, love a nap but heaved herself up and swung both legs over the side of the bed. A nap would leave her groggy.

The bathroom mirror displayed a garish reflection sporting eyeliner smudged down one pallid cheek and auburn sprigs going every which way. She grabbed a brush and smoothed the hair into a low ponytail before scrubbing off the makeup. Ten minutes later, she emerged with a fresh coat of mascara, rose-dusted pink cheeks, and a hint of a pinky red gloss.

A wardrobe change sounded nice, but the jeans and fuzzy red sweater she wore now would suffice. Tonight's dress was a bit much for the afternoon. Still, for a woman who'd recently taken to congratulating herself if she changed her pants more than twice a week, two outfits in one day constituted a stunning achievement.

She entered the hall and wrinkled her nose. An overpowering scent of cologne assaulted her senses, and she fought the urge to sneeze. The man exiting the room across from hers could probably be smelled through his closed door. Those beady black eyes sizing her up made her skin crawl.

"Good afternoon." He bent in a mock bow. "Bride or groom?"

"Bride," she answered. "Well, actually I don't know the bride. I'm here as my stepmom's plus one. And you?"

"The bride's my cousin." He hooked his thumbs through his belt loops and rocked back on his heels. "Tell ya the truth, though, I would've liked to skip the whole thing. But my uncle's not much for long drives anymore, so I let him talk me into it." He stepped forward and thrust out a hand. "I'm Colton."

A sandpaper-like palm engulfed hers. "Scarlett." She resisted the impulse to grimace. "Nice to meet you."

"After you." He swept the opposite hand toward the stairs.

Never having been one for small talk, she seized the

opportunity and followed the faint strains of music. She stepped onto the main floor and spotted Clarice waving to catch her attention.

Graham, bopping along to the music, nearly collided with another couple. He burst into a fit of laughter.

Maybe some of their exuberance would rub off on her.

"Aren't they wonderful?" Clarice gushed. "Get yourself some eggnog and join us."

"Uncle."

Scarlett glanced over her shoulder and cringed at the sight of Colton.

"Colton. There you are." Graham stopped dancing and flung out his arms. "Where were you all morning? I've already had lunch."

"Thought I'd catch up on some work before joining the fun."

"Well, while you've been working, I've made some new friends. Meet Clarice and Scarlett. Clarice and I are having a blast."

Clarice returned Colton's handshake. "A marvelous time. And you two must join us."

The band's next song lit up Graham's face, and he dashed Clarice back to the dance floor.

"Looks like my uncle's set his sights on your mom. We'll have to amuse ourselves." He pointed toward the bar. "I think I'll grab something to drink. Can I get you something? Is eggnog your thing?"

"No, thank you." She dropped onto the closest stool and didn't bother to correct him on her relationship with Clarice. The pep in his step spoke volumes of his excitement to kick off a few hours of day drinking. She couldn't care less and resolved to make it through the rest of the day. The fact no one else here dared to wear denim didn't help matters. Guests wouldn't don period costumes until the wedding, but everyone wore designer outfits costing more money than she used to make in a week. She spotted Wes holding court with three drooling women.

Yikes! Did he catch her staring? She swung her head in the opposite direction, but her peripheral vision showed him approach. Her stomach flip-flopped, irritating her to no end. After what he'd pulled last winter, she shouldn't give a rat's behind whether he paid her any attention.

"Hey." He rested an elbow on the cocktail table.

Behind him, Colton still waited at the bar in a throng of people.

"I meant to catch up with you earlier, but the day flew by." He slid out a stool and sat. "Any chance I could convince you to join me for a drink later tonight?"

"I don't think that's a good idea." A flurry of activity stirred in her stomach.

Clasping both hands together, he rested his forearms on the table. "One drink. I know I have some explaining to do. You don't owe me anything, but I'd really appreciate it if you'd hear me out."

She lifted an eyebrow and didn't keep the derision out of her voice. "I'm guessing Maisie's mother might not be so appreciative." Dead air filled the space between them.

Though he didn't flinch, he narrowed his gaze. "Maisie's mother is in England. We're not together."

Against her better judgment, she wanted to know what he had to say. If her night entailed lying awake and stewing, she deserved to have a solid reason. "What time will you be free?"

A small smile formed on his lips. "The rehearsal dinner ends at nine. At that point, the wedding party usually joins the other guests in the banquet hall. The event won't be as lavish as tomorrow night, but there'll be a live band, hors d'oeuvres, and drinks."

Hoping to appear more indifferent than she felt, she shrugged. "Then I suppose you'll know where to find me." Despite her best attempt at a stone-cold expression, seeing his relieved smile hit a nerve.

After clearing his throat, Colton deposited a ginger ale before her. He stuffed his free hand into a pocket and rocked back on his heels. "If I'd known someone else was joining us, I'd have chosen a bigger table."

Wes studied them for a moment and stood, nearly bumping into Vivian.

She dodged the collision and neared the table. "How's everyone doing?"

"Excellent." Colton raised his glass. "And hey, don't let Harper's prima donna demands get to you." He took a sip, swallowed, and faced Scarlett. "My cousin's got her knickers in a twist because she couldn't play dress-up today."

"Well, in her defense, we're dealing with an unfortunate turn of events." A tight smile hardened Vivian's pleasant features.

A flash of the bracelet fiasco earlier sprung to mind. "What do you mean?"

"The bride scheduled an appointment with our hairdresser for this afternoon to nail down a style for the wedding," Wes answered. "But Skylar slipped on some ice leaving her house and couldn't make it."

Was it her imagination, or was he avoiding eye

contact?

"It's worse than that," said Vivian. "She broke an ankle and won't be here tomorrow either."

"A damn travesty!" Colton threw his hands in the air.

Scarlett interrupted his bitter laugh. "Don't make fun of her, Colton. Perfect hair is on par with having the perfect dress for a bride. Some of my sweetest clients have morphed into total nightmares on their wedding day. The term Bridezilla doesn't begin to come close to the madness I've witnessed." At the unbridled hope on Vivian's face, she sucked in a breath. Now would be a good time for the floor to swallow her whole.

A server appeared bearing a tray of complimentary hors d'oeuvres.

With a thin sheen of sweat breaking out on his forehead, Colton brandished his near-empty glass in the air. "I'll have another." As he swung the glass, brown liquid sloshed onto the table. "And keep 'em coming."

The server flinched but left without saying another word.

Maybe this exchange would free Scarlett from Vivian's laser-focused stare. She watched Wes's mother purse her lips and glare at Colton. But sure enough, her gaze returned to Scarlett. A flock of geese took flight in her midsection.

"You're a hairdresser?"

No turning back now. She searched Wes's face for a lifeline but didn't see an ounce of empathy for the quicksand she'd just stepped into.

Vivian dragged over a chair from an adjacent table and perched on the edge with hands clasped deep in prayer. "Are you close to the bride? Is there any chance you'd be willing to help tomorrow?"

Maybe being unacquainted with the bride was the out she needed. "No, I've never even met her. I'm here as a plus one." *Wrong answer.*

At once, Vivian's gaze widened. "Even better. This way, if she's unhappy with your work, she can't hold the hair-*don't* over your head for the rest of your life." She scooched back in her seat and crossed her legs. "I'll make this job worth your while. We'll pay you Skylar's rate and comp your entire stay."

The quicksand deepened. She'd love to refuse Vivian's offer, but cutting Clarice's bill in half would be nice.

Colton leaned across the table and clamped a hand around her wrist. "Sounds like a deal. Even I'd be willing to tolerate Harper's attitude for a few hours if someone offered me a free weekend in return."

After scowling, Vivian bit her lip. "I'm sorry to put you on the spot like this. Take some time and think it over if you need to." She stood and joined her silent son.

If sacrificing her morning meant saving Clarice a few dollars, she'd do it. The kinder side of her felt for Vivian and even Harper. Oh, and given she couldn't remember the last time she'd received a paycheck, the extra cash might be nice. Wes didn't factor into the equation. Or so she told herself. "I don't need time. I'll do it." She wriggled her wrist from Colton's abrasive grip.

Vivian froze. She blinked once, released a breath, and blinked again. Her mouth curved into a smile. "Really?"

"Really. I'm happy to help." Vivian's bony arms wrapped around her. For a few eternal seconds, Scarlett's arms hung limp at her sides. Once she remembered to breathe, reflexes kicked in. With awkward hands, she patted the other woman's elbows.

After one final squeeze, Vivian released her hold. "I can't begin to thank you. Harper is scheduled for nine tomorrow. You could arrive at eight and get the lay of the land."

"I'll be there." She shifted her body toward the table and gripped her glass. Any future impromptu hugs should ensnare someone else.

A long, tapered fingernail pointed at Colton. "This one's a keeper, and don't you forget it."

"You don't need to sell me on that." He raised his glass in salute again. The empty glass hit the table with a clank.

Wes pursed his lips and lifted an eyebrow.

The server returned and, with a shaking hand, placed a fresh drink in front of Colton. "Wes…Viv." Trembling fingers fluttered to her neck and fidgeted with a silver chain. "We have a situation."

"Never a dull minute," Vivian said. "Please excuse us."

The unexpected weight of Wes's hand on her shoulder set off a fluttering in Scarlett's stomach. Thank goodness he made the gesture passing by and didn't notice her flaming cheeks. Thirteen-year-old girls exhibit less swoony reactions. She took a long sip from her straw, let the cool bubbles from the soda wash down her throat, and forced herself to regain a touch of poise.

"I wonder what the emergency is." Again, Colton cleared his throat. "Maybe they added pink roses to tomorrow's cake instead of red." He shrugged. "Kidding. They've got a lot going on here. Could be any number of things."

She spent the next hour vacillating between wishing Clarice would rejoin them to running through a slew of scenarios that could go down if she did meet Wes after the rehearsal. Colton droned on, oblivious to her lack of focus. If she nodded and smiled from time to time, he didn't require any further encouragement to continue talking about himself. She caught enough dribs and drabs to realize the size of his ego rocketed off the charts long ago. Had she ever met a man as enamored with himself?

The sight of Clarice and Graham approaching delivered the sweetest relief. She ignored the fact Colton was midsentence with yet another anecdote of his unmatched business acumen, stood, and clutched her purse. "You two must be tired after all that dancing. I heard a live band is playing tonight, too. You'll want to save some of your energy."

Clarice hooted. "Scarlett, you know me far better than that. When have these feet ever dared to resist a good beat?" She squeezed Graham's arm. "I will have to catch up with you tonight though. I'm just dying to try on my dress for tomorrow, and the manor's closet opens in fifteen minutes."

Another surge of relief flooded Scarlett. For a moment, she'd been afraid no end in sight existed to the mind-numbing torture of listening to Colton. If Clarice and Graham would wrap up their undying promises to meet later and find a way to tear themselves away from each other, then she could get the dress fitting over with and spend the rest of the afternoon preparing herself for the slew of excuses Wes might use to charm her.

On second thought, if she'd read the server's expression correctly, something major happened. Maybe Wes wouldn't have time at all for her tonight.

Chapter Four

The double doors to the manor's closet were already unlocked and thrown open. A more fitting description of this closet would be an ornate ballroom filled with racks of clothing. Scarlett would give anything for a peek inside the men's closet next door.

Despite originally bristling at The Timeless Manor's online catalog of rental clothing, she found herself looking forward to seeing her selection. Maybe she wouldn't need to resort to the fitted, strapless black dress packed as a backup. The line grew by the minute. Every woman staying at The Timeless Manor must have wanted to see their dress in person at the same time.

Two attendants in full period costume stood at the door, greeting guests and checking off names on a tablet.

When running a seamless business, some modern conveniences are too useful to forgo. Observations thus far proved technology sat at the top of the list.

A woman introduced as Eden escorted them to dressing rooms with gowns already hung inside.

"Now this is service," Clarice gushed.

At a minimum, Scarlett guessed the woman dressed in slim black pants and a snug black turtleneck stood at least six feet tall barefoot. She belonged on a runway.

Eden tossed the sleek, black ponytail off her shoulder, grinned, and pointed to a red button inside Clarice's dressing room. "I'll be back and forth. If you need any help at all and don't see me, just press that button, and I'll be back in a jiff."

The red velvet curtain closed. So, this incredible work of art was what these people called a dress. A ball gown in the truest sense of the word, made of deep burgundy fabric, filled the tight space. The corset hung on the opposite wall would not be happening. With featherlight fingertips, Scarlett slid the gown off its hanger and stepped inside as if climbing into a seven-tiered cake. Folds and flounces drifted to the floor. She shuffled out and gaped at her stepmother's transformation. Clarice stood resplendent in cascades of shimmering gold.

Both off-the-shoulder gowns featured square necklines ideal for showcasing a statement necklace.

"I'm speechless." Scarlett slid her hands down the satiny bodice.

"Well, you can lace me up while you find the words, and I'll do the same for you."

That task was easier said than done, but the effort paid off. Once finished, Scarlett swished behind Clarice toward a mirror spanning the back wall of the dressing room and joined a throng of chattering women.

"Well, hello, dress." Clarice turned and twisted, cooing at every angle.

With gentle hands, Scarlett hitched up several layers of material, released the fabric, and snorted. "You call this a dress?"

"How are we doing, ladies?" asked a voice from behind.

"Eden," breathed Clarice. "Where in the world does the manor find these gowns?"

"A fair amount of research goes into acquiring the

right items. I won't bore you with the gory details." She joined them in front of the mirror.

Clarice peered over her shoulder, checked out the rearview, and giggled. "I'm sorry, but I simply can't take my eyes off myself."

"I'm assuming you're both pleased?" Sculpted eyebrows soared toward the ceiling.

As Scarlett's gaze roved over the woman in red reflected in the mirror, tingling sparks traveled down her legs. Pleased? Pleased was a word better used to describe how a teacher felt about a student's behavior or effort. Even terms such as euphoric, floating on air, and spellbound didn't touch the surface of the thrill coursing through her soul. This dress was pure magic. "To say the least," she replied. "Let's get these back on their hangers so they remain pristine for tomorrow night."

With exaggerated reluctance, Clarice retreated behind her curtain to change.

Eden relayed instructions to retrieve their dresses between twelve and three the following day. Any earlier and they'd intrude on the wedding party.

Oh, to be a fly on the wall for that scene.

****

At almost 4:30, the late afternoon's setting sun darkened Wes's office. Not for the first time, he made a mental note to have brighter overhead lights installed. He sat alone at the antique Regency partner's desk and traced the lines of the smooth mahogany wood with an index finger. Unable to focus on the laptop displaying the guest list, he waited for the police to arrive to take a statement from the McKay family. He couldn't catch a break. First the bracelet disappeared. Now, one of the bridesmaids insisted her wallet was stolen. The one silver lining was Scarlett's agreement to work with the bridal party tomorrow.

Sunday morning couldn't come soon enough. The mother of the bride had the nerve to insinuate his seven-year-old daughter was responsible for the thefts. She called the behavior a cry for attention and insisted the child must feel neglected with her primary caretakers occupied day and night.

He rolled his shoulders, hoping to relieve the mounds of tension building every time he replayed her tinny, clipped voice in his head. Millie McKay didn't—couldn't—understand Maisie's love for this place and its events. She preferred shadowing him, her grandmother, and a few favored staff members throughout the day to attending playdates with other children. If Mrs. McKay knew how he'd struggled to make playtime a priority, she'd eat her words. He recognized the importance of Maisie finding enjoyment with her peers.

The door creaked open.

His mother's head poked through. "Got a minute?"

Wes closed the laptop. No sense wasting any more time pretending to pick apart the list of names eluding his attention. "Come in. Officer Delaney should be right behind you."

Vivian strode toward the desk and sat in one of the sleek, black leather guest chairs. "I have a theory," she said. "Do you think it's possible Mrs. McKay is responsible?"

Had he heard her correctly? What would Mrs. McKay gain from staging a bogus crime scene? He sat back, slack jawed. "Where is this idea coming from?"

"Hear me out." She inched to the edge of her seat. "What if she planned the thefts to get out of paying for the wedding?"

"I guess it's possible. But I don't see her as someone who wants anything less than a perfect weekend for her daughter."

"Just thinking outside the box." She lifted her chin. "One of my spontaneous ideas paid off earlier when I asked Scarlett Kerrigan to step in for Skylar."

"I can't argue with that fact." *Where was this line of thought going?*

"Pretty woman."

The mischievous smile playing around her lips ignited a fierce throbbing in his temples. "Can't argue with that statement either." He plucked an imaginary speck of lint from his tie, willing her to drop the Cupid act.

"I can't wait to see what she picked for a dress. With her delicate features and the right gown, she might upstage the bride."

Light rapping on the door stopped her musings.

"Sorry to interrupt." Officer Delaney hovered in the doorway.

Wes waved him in, resisting the overwhelming compulsion to express his gratitude. "No time like the present. I'll let the McKays know you're here."

One hour and one police report later, Wes escorted the officer to the lobby. He needed an aspirin to quell the pounding in his head. Mrs. McKay barely took a breath during a furious monologue about shattered expectations and dishonest staff. Without proof, her rant of accusations didn't add anything useful to the case. Little time remained before the wedding rehearsal. He hustled back to his office to put on a clean suit and freshen up. Right now, his appearance matched his frazzled nerves.

This armoire might be one of the best additions he'd made to the manor since taking over his father's office. Stashing a small wardrobe here saved him countless trips across town to his apartment. He changed into evening attire befitting nineteenth-century England and set aside today's suit for the dry cleaner.

He yearned for more time to mull over the best way to explain last year's upheaval to Scarlett. Entertaining the idea his words might be a year too late wasn't an option. How had he messed things up so horribly? Bad timing and worse choices. His divorce from Adrienne left him feeling like a failure. The trip to Aruba was supposed to snap him out of the slump he'd been existing in. He'd gone with the intention of enjoying time with friends but met Scarlett the first night.

Fun at first sight, not love, drew him in. He'd wanted to live in the moment. But by the end of their stay, he didn't want the moment to end and couldn't broach the subject of having an ex-wife and a child. Some topics should be discussed before anyone became emotionally invested. Cowardice set in, and by the time he arrived home, his life spun out of control. He'd finally pulled himself back together, but the apology planned for tonight might be too little too late.

****

At precisely six o'clock, a knock sounded on Scarlett's door. *Great*. Why was she never ready on time? She zipped up the side of her dress and pulled on one shoe at a time in a clumsy advance toward the door.

Clarice might be a whirling tornado in heels, but she was nothing if not prompt. She strolled in wearing a fresh hint of jasmine and a perfectly made-up face framed by glossy, dark waves. Time wreaked zero havoc on her figure, and the curve-hugging, red, sleeveless sheath showed off every minute of the hours spent working out. "Gorgeous as ever." Scarlett stepped aside. "One of these days, I might get over my loathing for strenuous activity and accept your open-ended offer to use a guest gym pass."

"You're biased."

On a normal day, flattery was wasted on her stepmother. Clarice sought only her own approval. But she wasn't immune to a sincere compliment after making an extra effort to gussy up. As she strode toward the dresser, the sway of her hips indicated that tonight was one of those occasions. "We both know Graham won't notice another woman in the room tonight."

Clarice stepped back on one red, spiked heel and flung a hand to her hip. "I'll tell you what. If he does, I'll just pop a few more of those lemon squares."

Lemon squares? "What are you talking about?"

Gasping, Clarice fluttered a hand to her throat. "I meant to tell you earlier. When Wes first told me, I assumed he was pulling my leg."

"Told you what?"

"The lemon squares are enchanted." She waggled a finger and perched on the edge of the bed. "Don't look at me like that. He insisted the pastry chef here uses an old Celtic recipe that works like some sort of love potion. Anyone who eats a square will attract romance into his or her life. And let me tell you, I no sooner dropped the last bite of that lemony goodness into my mouth, and Graham appeared at our table."

Wes had found Clarice's sweet spot. She adored all things mystical. Scarlett drew a short breath and sighed. "Well, if any truth to that exists, I wish I'd skipped mine earlier. I could do with a break from romance."

"If memory serves, just after lunch, I spotted you with Colton hot on your heels." She stood and smoothed her dress. "What we both need is for you to finish getting ready so we can be on our way."

Glad to put an end to the conversation, Scarlett entered the powder room and ran a brush through her hair one final time. Managing this mane was a futile effort at best. Her hair had a mind of its own, regardless of effort and professional expertise. But tonight, the amber waves fell smooth over her shoulders and enhanced her creamy complexion. Only a slumped posture revealed evidence of someone who'd spent an eternity in a car, eaten too large of a lunch, and now bore the leaden weight of exhaustion.

Whoever invented forgiving jersey material deserved a medal. Without it, the black, tulip hem dress risked an unflattering fit. The long sleeves offset her bare legs and provided a dash of modesty for an otherwise skimpy choice. Balancing on a pair of patent leather, black stilettos, she scrutinized her already cramping feet. Was she standing on needles or heels? No telling how long she'd last in them, but the discomfort might be worthwhile. They sure did wonders for the calves. She emerged with shoulders pushed back, slipped on a wristlet, and teetered out the door. Not even Clarice's huffs and mutters about punctuality could diffuse her spark of confidence.

Voices and laughter drifted up the stairs from a foyer animated by guests, embracing an old-world holiday spirit. The police officer, escorted to the front door by a grim Wes, did not belong in this picture-perfect scene.

After his departure, Wes turned his gaze to the foyer

with deep lines etched across his forehead. He stalked past nearby spectators and rounded the corner without a word to anyone.

"Wonder what that to-do was all about," Clarice mused. "Anyhoot, let's go find ourselves a table."

The urge to follow Wes tugged with the force of a super magnet. Before she could determine whether to blame concern or sheer nosiness, flailing arms drew her attention to Graham and Colton seated at a table for four. "I believe you're being summoned."

Clarice dragged her gaze from the overflowing buffets and spotted Graham. "Would you look at that? I insisted he not revolve his evening around our schedule. But I told him we'd be eating at six thirty, and he's right on time. I guess we won't be dining alone."

Coffee better be on the menu if she faced another few hours of Colton extolling his personal virtues. At least Graham's and Clarice's excitement lightened her mood. And they'd balance out the conversation.

The last one to arrive after hitting the buffets, Clarice sat to the tune of Graham's whistle.

He goggled at her plate. "Do you always eat like this?"

Grinning, she lowered her chin. "I'll let you in on my secret. I don't snack, and I love working up a good sweat. It's as simple as that."

"What about dessert?" Graham asked.

"I adore dessert. Dinner should always end with a sweet treat."

He snorted. "Whatever works."

Dinner passed better than expected with Graham sharing what seemed a million funny anecdotes about the bride's family. Once again, the food was superb. Scarlett took a final bite of baked stuffed shrimp. The sweet shellfish breaded with a crabmeat stuffing burst with flavor. She considered a second helping before checking out the mini dessert bar.

"Well, I'm glad to see everyone having a wonderful time."

She peered over her shoulder at Wes.

Inches away, he stood with one hand on the back of her chair. "Can I get you anything?"

A bit more time to brace myself for these impromptu appearances might be nice. "We're just finishing. I thought you were at the rehearsal dinner."

"I am. Well, I was. But I always check in here from time to time as well."

His intense stare left her breathless. In that moment, no one else sat at the table.

"I hope you're still planning to stay for the band?"

"Wouldn't miss it," interjected Graham.

Wes's head jerked up. He offered a small smile and a curt nod, then his full attention settled on her once again. "I look forward to seeing you later this evening."

With the sleek stride of a cat and the charm of the smoothest politician, he strode to the next table. Riveted by the starry-eyed guests who greeted him with the same reverence one might expect to be reserved for royalty, she exerted every ounce of strength to stop staring. She struggled to follow the interrupted conversation and met a narrowed gaze fixed on her.

"Would you excuse us?" Clarice batted her lashes at Graham and Colton. "We really should powder our noses before the party gets started." She promised to find them later and hustled Scarlett out of the dining room. Once out of view, Clarice coaxed her onto a plush settee in the foyer. "Spill it." She arched back and threw up her hands. "Oh, no. Don't give me that I-don't-know-what-you're-talking-about face. When you realized who stood behind you, your expression revealed all. And I'm not buying for one second that he often leaves rehearsal dinners to check in on the regular dining room." A hand gestured toward several employees passing by. "He has plenty of staff to take care of such things, and the bride and groom are paying one pretty penny for his undivided attention."

Clarice knew her better than anyone. She'd never escape this weekend without coming clean. And let's face it, she could use the ear. She breathed in the fragrant scent of the poinsettias flanking each end of the seat. "Remember that trip I took to Aruba last winter?"

Both eyebrows shot up. "That's the guy you met? The one you spent your entire trip with and never heard from again?"

At her incredulous tone, Scarlett slumped and nodded. "Until we went off the road this afternoon, and he played guardian angel."

Clarice's gaze soared toward the ceiling. She slumped with a groan. "How many times have I told you it's never a good idea to date someone prettier than you are?"

No one knew how to make her laugh at the most ridiculous times better than this woman. She clasped one of Clarice's hands. "You always did know just the right thing to say."

"What's he doing here?"

The pitying expression accompanying Clarice's returned squeeze sparked a twinge of regret. Maybe she should have saved this tale of woe for the drive home. Clarice deserved a drama-free weekend, not a three-day stint playing therapist to her stepdaughter venting about being burned yet again. She'd never let the subject drop now. "I don't know. But he and his mother work for the manor."

"Who's his mother?" Her brow furrowed.

"I think she said her name is Vivian."

Clarice's eyes bulged, and her mouth dropped open. "Vivian? The Vivian Harley who owns this place?"

A woman stopped next to the settee and checked her phone.

Scarlett lifted a finger to her lips and jutted her chin toward the tall brunette. This conversation was on hold until they had a bit more privacy. Scarlett fumed. Another thing he failed to be truthful about. What his mother did or didn't own wasn't any of her business. But he'd told her he worked for a resort and spa in Portsmouth then turned up at one of the most successful family-owned venues in New England. Now she learned he's a member of that family. Did he think she was a gold digger?

Once they were alone, Clarice slid closer. "Has he given any indication as to why he cut you off?"

With a sigh, Scarlett tucked a lock of hair behind one ear. "He wants me to meet him tonight. I think he wants to explain." Shrewd, espresso eyes peered into her own and read her heart.

Clarice straightened. "You're still carrying a torch."

Until now, herculean efforts to snuff out any lingering flames allowed her to languish in the sweet world of denial. Clarice didn't believe in blissful ignorance, and she didn't know how to mince words. With one comment, she leveled Scarlett with a heaping dose of reality. "You think I should put him off?"

"I didn't say that. Absolutely hear him out if for nothing more than to get some closure on the matter."

"That's what I'm thinking." She paused and worked up the nerve to spill the rest of the truth. "But what if I told you he has a daughter and never mentioned her once in Aruba?" The other guests passing by, the chatter, and the music faded away while this little tidbit sunk in. With her lips forming a tight "W," perhaps for the question "wife" or "what in the world did you just say," Clarice stared unblinking.

"Is a wife waiting for him at home?"

"He claims they're not together." The classic line rang false to her own ears. "I want to know if he was married last year." She braced herself for one of Clarice's signature barbs.

Instead, she smirked and patted her knee. "Just don't allow yourself to be sucked into a swoon fest weekend by a chiseled chin."

"Hah! Been there, done that." Scarlett stood. If history was any indication, this conversation dangled on the cusp of rolling into a lecture. "We should go. You don't want to keep your new friend waiting."

Soon enough, she'd have all the facts. Well, assuming Wes chose full honesty over withholding key details. What could he say to rebuild her trust? Why couldn't she shake the need for him to want her back? She despised the part of herself that craved a forgivable story and a new start.

Chapter Five

Led by the luminous Harper and a man who Scarlett presumed to be her fiancé, the wedding party trickled into the main dining hall from the rehearsal dinner. A thundering heartbeat roared in her ears. She racked her brain for a way to politely extricate herself from the table.

The longer he sat, the more drinks Colton drained.

By nine, she still hadn't spotted Wes. A little planning might have helped. They should have designated a time and place to meet.

Colton draped one arm over the back of her chair and leaned forward.

Alcohol-infused breath wafted into her face and provided the final incentive to put an end to dinner. She tossed her napkin on the table, ignoring his confused, yet numb expression. "Clarice, I'll catch up with you in a bit. I need to stretch my legs."

"I'll keep you company." Colton attempted to stand but swayed and dropped back into his seat.

"No need." She smiled with the reassurance he'd be in no rush to follow, turned to leave, but stopped short. The scorching fingers of humiliation crept up her neck and over her cheeks.

Wes stood across the room, watching.

A quick scan of the room confirmed guests at every table dined with refinement despite a few cocktails. Was

175

she now a victim of guilt by association due to Colton's intoxication? She swallowed her embarrassment and maneuvered around the tables, guests, and stray chairs in her path. As she approached him and his sour expression, the din of voices, laughter, and music faded into a blurry background.

"Your date's a real charmer."

Date? Her first instinct was to correct him. But on second thought, the presumption she'd accompanied Colton might have an advantage. Aside from his current sloppy state, general lack of personality, and beady eyes, he wasn't bad looking. Maybe if she pretended he was her boyfriend, she'd be less inclined to fall victim to Wes's games. "What did you want to talk about? I already agreed to style the bride's hair tomorrow, so you don't need to go through the motions of being nice to convince me to help out."

His lips formed a thin line. "Just come with me."

The band's next song filled the dance floor with guests so engrossed in their moves they were oblivious to anyone attempting to make their way through the crowd.

Wes placed a hand on the small of her back, sending an unappreciated yet warming shiver down her spine, and guided her out of the room. She knew she should ask him to remove his hand, but the slight lump forming in her throat stole her words. For a moment, she slipped back to a time when such intimacies between them were taken for granted.

The foyer led to a dim sitting room, lit with wall sconces and a blazing fire.

A handful of people engaged in subdued conversations sat scattered about on couches and chairs.

Wes chose two empty club chairs in a corner and sat forward with elbows resting on his thighs. "Let me dive right in and apologize."

She shrugged. "I don't want an apology. I want the truth. When you were in Aruba, were you married?"

"I wasn't."

Her heart skittered an erratic beat, inducing a lightheaded sensation. *And now, the million-dollar question…* "Why didn't you mention Maisie?"

He broke eye contact while reaching up and loosening his tie. "I should have. By the end of the week, I'd let too much time go by without saying something."

"And so you blew me off after we left. Much easier than coming clean." The hurt that should have died a year ago sank its claws into her chest. She fumed in silence, waiting for him to plot a solid defense.

He lowered his head and rubbed the back of his neck. "Things kind of spun out of control. I'd just arrived at the airport, and my mom called to tell me my dad passed unexpectedly." He paused. The muscles in his jaw tensed.

The pained expression taking over his face pummeled Scarlett with the memory of losing her own father. She was all too familiar with the state of shock that followed the unexpected loss of one of the most significant people in your life. The heartbreak ebbed and flowed with the passage of time, but always clung to the soul, just waiting for the perfect moment to engulf its host with a mind-numbing surge of sorrow.

"By the time I got here, Adrienne and Maisie were waiting."

Applause erupted on the opposite side of the room, and several stray notes rang from a piano. Guests surrounded the pianist and shouted requests until a few familiar notes introduced a crowd pleaser.

"Sorry about that. Our pianist likes to rile up the crowd." Wes rubbed his palms along his thighs. "I'll make a long story short. Adrienne took over in the best possible way. The woman is nothing if not efficient, and my mom and I weren't in the right frame of mind to handle arrangements. Adrienne was with me every step of the way and…" He paused and swallowed. "For a short time, I thought we'd get back together."

Over the last year, she'd conjured countless possible explanations for his behavior. But she never expected to hear a story like this one. "I'm sincerely sorry about your father." Much of the previous hostility left her voice. "You could've said something."

"I should have."

Another couple settled on the Queen Anne love seat across from them.

Some people do not know how to read a room. With all the available, cozy seating, they chose a spot in direct earshot of a private conversation. Scarlett didn't need an audience for the words burning the edge of her tongue. Bristling at the intrusion and desperate for somewhere else to sit, she darted her gaze around the room. But the server from this afternoon diverted her attention.

Curiosity bloomed. Why were the police here earlier? Did their arrival have something to do with the late afternoon emergency? "Then we agree, and this subject has outworn its welcome. So, let's change it. Who called the police today?"

Wes sat back with a deep sigh. "One of the bridesmaids reported her wallet stolen. With another potential theft on the heels of the missing bracelet, the

McKay family called them."

"Geez, should I be concerned?" Not that she owned much worth stealing, but Clarice always traveled with a few pieces of pricey jewelry.

"I hope not." With lips pursed, he glanced at the nearby couple then scooted to the edge of his seat. "We've never had anything of value disappear."

Attempting to match his lowered voice, she reduced her volume. "Do you have any new staff members?"

"Only my cousin, Larson." He shook his head. "But he's not a thief. My money's on someone in the wedding party or on the guest list."

An image of Larson hauling her luggage flashed through her mind. His shy, eager-to-please demeanor didn't strike her as a mere façade for a criminal. She bit her lip and fidgeted with the ribbon pendant attached to the gold chain around her neck. "Do you have any clues to work with?" The frustration clouding his face answered for him.

"The mother of the bride insists my cousin was present on both occasions. But she'd already taken an instant dislike to him at check-in. She kicked off her weekend by complaining he'd manhandled her luggage. When the bracelet disappeared, he was the first one she pointed a finger at."

The couple sitting nearby lacked the manners to hide the fact they now hung on Wes's every word. Scarlett glared at them. "Well, I hope you solve the mystery before the weekend is over."

"Me, too. The family is threatening to withhold payment. That bracelet cost thousands. If bad publicity becomes a factor, I'm not confident we'll recoup the loss. Not with such a high-profile wedding."

Since they'd arrived, the room grew crowded. At this rate, everyone on the guest list would have a front row seat to the inside scoop on the unsolved mysteries. She didn't have a good reason to stay any longer. He blew her off a year ago and finally provided an explanation. Withholding the fact he had a child and then reunited with his wife was inexcusable. Even if her heart did go out for the loss of his father.

On the bright side, she could view their fling as a learning opportunity. She'd never again allow herself to be blinded by beautiful bone structure spewing empty promises in the midst of a whirlwind romance. If the last year taught her anything, experience dictated a much-needed break from relationships. Her self-esteem might not withstand another blow. "I should check on Clarice." She stood.

"And I should see how everything is going for the bride and groom." He followed her out of the sitting room and into the foyer.

This time, he kept his hands to himself. As Scarlett neared the ballroom, she spotted Clarice and Graham. They'd hit the dance floor and appeared to be there for the long haul.

Clarice shimmied.

Graham bobbed up and down out of beat with the band.

"I don't think you were missed." Wes nudged her with an elbow and laughed.

Colton emerged from the center of the crowd. Inebriated, he swayed and stumbled from one woman to the next in failed attempts to engage a partner.

The smile forming on her face faltered. A mix of disbelief and dread nailed her to the floor. At the thought of becoming the next victim subjected to his slobbering, she shuddered. "I can't go back in there," she said, more to herself than Wes.

He shifted his gaze and furrowed a brow.

She'd spoken aloud? Heat rose up her neck and spilled onto her cheeks. Sheer embarrassment forced out the truth. "That guy? Not my date."

"But—"

"I never said he was. You jumped to conclusions, and I went with it. I didn't want you thinking I'd be an easy target." She flitted a hand in the air. "Fool me once and all that."

His mouth twitched. "Whatever your status is, I have a feeling he'll be happy to see you."

She gripped his arm, a vise tightening her chest. "He *can't* see me."

Colton swayed closer to the room's entrance.

Without warning, Wes grabbed her hand and pulled her out of sight, down a hallway, and into the kitchen.

Adrenaline surged through her veins. The door swung closed, and she burst into a fit of laughter. She doubled over to catch her breath, grateful the staff zipping about in a frenzy was too busy to spare an ounce of attention on a woman running for her life.

Some employees cleaned up from dinner. Others chopped vegetables and worked over the stove stirring steaming pots and sautéing celery, onions, and garlic. The cacophony of voices, clanging pans, and clattering plates was dulled by the medley of aromas reinvigorating her appetite.

Her presence didn't register as even a minor interruption on anyone's radar. She wiped her eyes and inhaled a deep breath. She needed to regain some semblance of control. "Thanks."

"Sorry, I was impulsive." Sucking in a breath, he locked his hands behind his head. "But I have a feeling your dinner companion will stumble upstairs to bed sooner than later. You can wait in here and then join the party."

She glanced around. "Will I be in the way?"

"Probably." Fine lines crinkled from the corners of his eyes. "But no one will care. You can get a preview of what's on the menu for tomorrow."

Still elated by the narrow escape, she agreed and figured endorphins could be blamed for the poor judgment. The entertainment provided by the kitchen staff performing a well-practiced, technical dance also shared some of the responsibility.

"How about a tour?" He gestured toward a counter lined with giant casserole pans filled with side dishes. "Here we have all the extras. We'll also serve prime rib, turkey, and sole. But those won't be seen to 'til morning." He hooked a thumb over his shoulder toward another counter. "I think that's more your speed."

The sly grin sliding across his face sent her pulse pounding. He remembered her sweet tooth. Desserts filled every square inch with one glorious cake in the center. "I'd like to pull up a chair and grab a fork, but I wouldn't know where to begin. What kind of cake is that?" She stepped closer. A three-tiered masterpiece dripping with orange blossoms made of icing loomed before her.

"Traditionally, fruitcakes were served with similar scrolling and orange blossoms. But the bride wanted a standard white cake. Therefore, we have the image she's going for and the taste."

Scarlett roved her gaze over the miniature treats: shortbread cookies, chocolate-covered strawberries, and lemon tarts to name a few. Several large apple tarts and mince pies were also on display. She breathed in the intoxicating scent of sugar, her mouth watering with anticipation. "This counter is a sugar addict's heaven. Who'll have room for cake with all of these delectable tidbits?"

A plump pastry chef, storing the items, laughed and spun around. A few strands of honey-streaked hair had slipped out of her bun, and a sheen of perspiration glistened on her reddened cheeks. "Harper wants the full experience. That package includes a champagne-infused, multicourse meal followed by tea and a large dessert selection. The cake will most likely go home with guests in individual boxes. I need to get some of these goodies into the fridge." She lifted two trays.

The removal of the trays piled high with apple tarts revealed adorable desserts aligned in rows on cookie sheets. "What are those?" Scarlett enunciated each word.

"Tea cake cookies," Wes replied.

"I've never seen anything like them before. They're too pretty to eat." She marveled over the intricate detail of the unique cookies. Each was molded into the shape of an elaborate Victorian hat in a variety of vibrant colors.

"Maybe, but you'd be missing out. The top of the hat is a delicious lemon pound cake, and the bottom is a soft, sweet biscuit." Both hands moved to his stomach. For a moment, he squeezed his eyes shut. "Almost like a ladyfinger."

"Hands off the tea cakes, Wes," teased the voice from behind the refrigerator door.

He chuckled. "Ivy has a side business selling these. She has more orders than she can fill."

The refrigerator door closed, and Ivy bustled to the counter. "You might have heard of southern tea cakes or maybe Russian tea cakes. This recipe is meant to be the English version, but my interpretation is not historically accurate. Still, these little hats are far more adorable than the typical flat cookie, and I haven't received any complaints yet."

Scarlett studied the details on each. "Why do they have long, red ribbons poking out?"

Wes slid his thumb and index finger along one piece of the satin fabric. "The ribbon is attached to a charm hidden in the center. Each charm has a special meaning. Like, a penny for wealth, a flower for a blossoming relationship, or a horseshoe for good luck—to name a few."

"Your seating card will include the list of charms and their meanings, so don't toss it after you've found your table." Ivy reached back and tightened her apron.

"I won't. Thank you." This little tradition was something to look forward to. How had she never heard of such a custom before? Clarice was in for a real surprise.

"Let's get out of Ivy's way. If you're interested, the atrium is beautiful this time of year."

She wasn't ready to chance a peek into the ballroom yet. Colton might not have retired for the night, and her renewed energy demanded an outlet better than the isolation offered by her empty room. Despite discovered shortcomings and intolerable prior behavior, Wes was easy to be with. At least he'd finally laid bare the truth for her to digest.

After a warm goodbye to Ivy, Scarlett followed Wes out of the kitchen and strolled toward the farthest end of the manor. Decorations from Christmases past glittered around her until she reached an open space resembling a room encased in glass. Twinkling fairy lights and several trees illuminated the room, creating a candle-lit effect. Miniature displays of wintery towns evoked festive warmth. A small bar offering drinks and appetizers stood in the hallway, preserving the pristine architecture of the atrium with its pitched, soaring ceiling.

Wes took two glasses of champagne and gestured toward an open divan.

But the windows with a view of the property drew Scarlett forward. The back lawn rolled flat to a stone wall overlooking a lake. Even in the dark, the moon and outside lamp posts offered enough light to take away her breath. "Gorgeous," she whispered. Her fingertips on the cool glass provided a welcoming chill and balanced the warmth radiating between them.

"That view is the main reason we're booked solid spring through fall for weddings and events." He handed her a champagne flute and took a sip from his own. "Once the warmer weather sets in, maybe you'd consider making another trip to New Hampshire." He stepped closer. "I think you'd really enjoy it."

Each velvet word caressed her ear and drifted down her neck. She inhaled the delicate bouquet from her glass, then sipped her champagne. As the fine bubbles burst on her tongue with an underlying hint of pear, she prayed for a touch of liquid courage before responding with the one nagging question. "Is Maisie's mother in the picture at all?" She locked her gaze on the grounds, knowing his expression might reveal something she didn't want to see.

"Adrienne is not even in the country."

Fear, or maybe hope, churned her insides. No telling which force was stronger.

Chapter Six

Scarlett followed Wes's gaze toward a couple vacating two seats by one of the atrium's arched windows.

"Can we sit?" Moments later, he dragged a chair closer and took a breath. "I don't have any bad feelings toward Adrienne. In fact, I have nothing but good things to say about her." He shrugged. "We were never right for each other and should've learned that lesson the first time we split up."

"What happened?" Maybe she shouldn't have asked, but something in his tone stirred a desire to hear the full story.

"Our moms have been friends since childhood. You can imagine how elated they were when our friendship led to romance. I think, once that line was crossed, Adrienne felt trapped." He sucked in a breath and stared out the window. "I know I did."

"So, you got married?" Scarlett shook her head. "Did you love each other?"

He shifted back his gaze. "Yeah, but we wanted different things. Adrienne wasn't meant to be tied to this town or me. Maisie's arrival didn't change that fact. She'd wanted to escape for decades and seized the first viable opportunity. Her home base was Hemlock Bend. But when traveling for work, she left Maisie with her parents or mine." He paused and stared into his champagne flute. "Even though the divorce was smooth, as far as these things go, I felt like a failure. Every soul in this tiny town obsessed over what brought down the perfect couple. I accepted a position managing a resort and spa in Portsmouth, packed up, and left."

"The move must have been hard on Maisie." She bit back the choice words she had for Adrienne and laid a hand on his arm. "And you."

"I missed her like crazy. Weekend trips home weren't enough." He pinched the air with his thumb and forefinger. "I was this close to quitting and moving back home before my dad died. Adrienne was never here, and Maisie deserved to have at least one parent present most of the time. My dad's passing served as the catalyst I needed to make the move." He pressed a hand to his chest. "I never expected Adrienne to stick around. But she checked in on my mom daily."

A server passing hors d'oeuvres stopped and extended a tray of mini crab cakes.

Usually, Scarlett would snatch at least two. But the leaden weight sitting in her stomach forced a slight shake of the head. She swallowed over the lump forming in her throat. "You knew she was also checking in on you?"

"Not at first." He rubbed the back of his neck and leaned forward. "I'd taken over my father's role at the manor and didn't give her visits much thought. But eventually, we fell into a comfortable routine, and I thought our relationship was back on track. Until, of course, Adrienne received a job offer she couldn't turn down."

"Couldn't or wouldn't?" She let out a short breath. "Sorry. Go on."

"You're right. She had a choice to make." Leaning

back, he sighed. "And she chose to take off for Europe while Maisie stayed in New Hampshire. It might sound selfish for her to up and go. But the new job required working around the clock. I choose to see her decision to leave our daughter with me as selfless. Maisie feels secure and loved. Even by a mom halfway across the world." He took another sip of champagne and sat the empty flute on the windowsill. "Maybe if I'd been in love with her, the split would've stung more. Instead, I felt like a good friend left town but stayed in touch."

"Maisie's lucky to have parents who support each other even after a divorce." Scarlett shifted in her seat, crossed her legs, and allowed one shoe to dangle from her toes. Her cramped foot arched in sweet relief.

"Get to know her a little better." He cocked his head to one side and grinned. "You'll know we're the lucky ones."

Hours ticked by filled with stories and anecdotes from the past year. Scarlett shared a brief overview of her recent upsets and described losing her job and becoming financially dependent on her ex-boyfriend. "The next blow hit when Niall asked me to pack my things and move out after proposing to a woman he'd long insisted was just a friend." She picked at a chipped nail, then dropped her hands into her lap. "Rock bottom swallowed me whole."

Talking about the breakup dredged up the recurring pit in her stomach that formed every time she relived the hurt and humiliation. She waved away Wes's scowl with a flick of her hand. "It's fine though. Once the holidays are over, I'm broadening my job search and will take whatever I can get. I can only mooch off Clarice for so long before I won't stand the sight of myself."

"I'm sorry you've had such a rough year." His forehead creased above eyebrows drawn together.

"Oh, please. You haven't had an easy few months either."

Scarlett shifted her gaze toward Clarice entering the atrium on Graham's arm like the belle of the ball.

"Where in the world have you been all night?" Clarice asked.

"Getting the grand tour. Have you been enjoying yourself?"

Clarice giggled. "Graham, have we been enjoying ourselves?"

"Sure have," he said. "Colton abandoned his search for you eons ago and retired to his room."

Feigning disappointment with a groan, Scarlett scrunched up her face. "I'm sure our paths will cross tomorrow."

With a snort, Clarice wrinkled her nose. "Well, let's hope he's in better shape by morning." She surveyed the room, then turned toward Wes. "Who's in charge of decorating this place? Absolutely nothing has been overlooked."

"My mother does most of it," Wes replied. "And, trust me, you haven't seen anything yet. Tomorrow will blow you away. You will literally feel like you've stepped into late 1800s Victorian England."

"I have one question though." Clarice held up a finger. "Was tinsel invented prior to the Victorian era? I haven't seen a single strand."

"It existed." A hint of pink crept over Wes's cheeks. "But my mother's not a fan, so we don't use it."

Clarice tapped her chin with a cherry red fingertip. "I could see how a few errant strands on the floor or furniture might make more work for the staff, but I've always found tinsel festive. And I know Scarlett agrees with me."

Did she always have to be so blunt? "What gave you that impression? I know many people think the silver is too much and takes away from the tree. To each their own."

"Of course, but you and I both know you noted the lack of tinsel on the tree in your room."

True, she might have noticed, but she hadn't breathed a word to Clarice. "I didn't notice anything other than its beauty."

Wes laughed and thrust his palms in the air. "Hey, maybe you're on to something. Maybe we should survey guests before they arrive and ask what they'd prefer to see on their tree."

"Don't be ridiculous." Scarlett shook her head. "You shouldn't change a thing."

"I agree." Clarice grinned and patted his arm. "I'm just giving her a hard time." The low whistle of a train diverted her focus to a display along several windows. A miniature Christmas train began its ride over the tracks and followed a ledge circling the room. "Oh, I need to get a closer look." She made a beeline for the tracks.

Graham shuffled after her, barely keeping up.

"Dance with me?"

Knowing this situation might end far from well, she took Wes's hand and allowed him to lead the way. Swaying, lost in the music and memories of the last time he'd held her in his arms, her heart ached for everything they'd lost this year.

His head dipped, and firm lips fell on hers. The jolts of electricity storming through her body left her balancing on legs of butter. A faraway voice screamed to break away, but her champagne-infused head ignored the warning. The last notes of the song played out, and she drew back as if waking from a dream. "I should go."

Wes leaned forward. "Stay a little longer."

Tempted beyond reason, she forced herself to refuse. Hadn't she sworn off men for the immediate future? Her throat tightened, making it difficult to swallow. "I'd better return to my room. I have an early morning, and I'm sure you have guests to attend to." Her desire for one last dance was mirrored in the disappointment shadowing his features.

He released her. "I'll see you at eight?"

The music and animated voices surrounding her grew deafening. A blanket of cold claimed residence where his arms had been. For no good reason, tears stung the back of her eyes. Tomorrow, she'd skip the champagne. Seized with a desperate need to flee before she made a fool of herself, she managed a curt nod and left him standing alone. Hustling down the hall, she wasn't sure if her pounding heart meant she hoped he'd follow or leave her alone.

****

A shrill, incessant ring increased in volume with each effort to break through the fog of a restless sleep. With eyes glued shut, Scarlett flopped an arm across the bed and groped for the offending receiver. After thanking the front desk, she heaved herself to a sitting position. Good thing she'd requested a wake-up call. The chiming alarm from her cell phone failed to accomplish the task.

An extra hour of sleep would have been a gift. She'd tossed and turned all night alternating replays of her conversation with Wes and admonitions to herself to forget the whole encounter. If she couldn't make things last with a guy who lived five miles away, how could she expect this relationship to work? She'd left Aruba believing they formed enough of a connection to pursue a long-distance relationship. Enough happened since then to reveal how naïve she'd been. She dragged herself out of bed, into the shower, and down to the salon in less than an hour.

Wes waited with a cup of coffee and a plate offering a scrumptious blueberry muffin, fruit, and several strips of bacon. "Did you eat?"

"I figured I'd grab something later." Her stomach rumbled at the scent of bacon overpowering the original essence of shampoo and hairspray.

"Well, keep the dish handy in case you get a break and need a snack. You'll want to keep up your energy with this morning's clientele."

"Thank you." She accepted the coffee and took a sip. The creamy warmth moving down her throat forced her eyes closed. "You remembered." On the verge of sinking to the floor and savoring every last drop, she fluttered open her lashes.

"Splash of cream, one sugar."

Maisie bounded into the salon, blonde curls bouncing with each step. "Can I stay and watch? Myra always used to let me watch the ladies get their hair done."

The momentary flicker of caffeine-induced ecstasy screeched to a halt. Taken aback by the girl's complete lack of timidity, Scarlett blinked a few times to process the request. "Absolutely. My name is Scarlett. In fact, I could use an extra pair of hands in here this morning. I'm

193

new, and I'm not quite sure where everything is."

"Oh, I know where *everything* is." Maisie hopped from one foot to the other. "You tell me if you need something, and I'll get it."

Scarlett met Wes's smile. "If it's okay with your dad."

"No argument from me, if you're sure you don't mind." He tugged one of Maisie's curls. "Just don't be underfoot."

She rolled her eyes and giggled.

"I'll leave you two to it." After planting a kiss on his daughter's head, he strode out.

Scarlett's few remaining minutes to prepare flew by in a blur. Before she knew it, seven women blew into the salon in a whirlwind of activity. As usual, Harper stood out in the crowd with her unique beauty and larger-than-life personality.

She pointed at Scarlett with both hands. "You're doing me first. I didn't get my practice run yesterday, and if you take the whole freakin' morning to get my hair perfect, so be it." She flicked a bracelet-laden wrist toward the other women. "If we run out of time, my dear ladies here can be left to their own devices."

"Don't worry. Everyone's hairdressing needs will be met." Despite promises made, Scarlett offered a silent prayer one of the ideas she'd saved on her phone would meet approval.

Harper narrowed choices to an elaborate up-do with delicate tendrils falling in perfect frame to her face. A few carefully placed sparkling pins and voila…stunning bride.

The long-held sigh of relief threatening to escape her lungs evaporated. The bride turned out to be a much easier customer than expected.

Maisie proved herself to be invaluable. How old was she? No matter, the girl knew this salon inside and out. Her unabashed gushing over Harper's hair solidified how the bride already felt about herself.

"You're an absolute artist, Scarlett. Expect to hear from me in the future." Gripping a hand mirror, Harper twisted before the mirror spanning the wall. "If you ladies will excuse me, I'm retreating to my bridal suite for a head start on makeup. Pop upstairs as soon as you can."

The door swung closed, and the room stilled in deafening silence. Stares darted from one face to another before a roar erupted with everyone speaking at once.

Scarlett continued working on the current head of hair in front of her without breathing a word to indicate she paid an ounce of attention to their conversation. The effort to maintain an expression of disinterest while they chattered away required tremendous strength. She stole a few glances at Maisie, who busied herself with color coordinating the display of nail polish bottles. With everyone speaking at once, Scarlett struggled to follow the conversation. Something was wrong…more than wrong.

The wedding bands had disappeared.

Several women speculated the theft happened last night. But with so few clues available, no one could be sure. Mrs. McKay's diamond bracelet and a bridesmaid's wallet were still missing. Without a probable suspect, the entire staff remained under suspicion.

"The thief is definitely someone on the guest list." The maid of honor stared at her friends through the mirror.

"I don't believe that for a minute." Across the salon, a bridesmaid trailed her fingers along a shelf of hair products. "Everyone adores Harper. Who would want to ruin this weekend?"

A memory of Colton spewing venomous statements about his cousin popped into Scarlett's brain. He didn't adore Harper in the least. She tuned out the drone of voices and attempted to recall his exact words.

Maisie thrust a pink nail polish bottle in the air. "When we're finished, can I borrow this one? You could paint my nails. I want to surprise my mommy."

Her mommy? Her mommy lived in Europe. On second thought, she'd probably be calling on a video call of some kind. "Sure, you can hold up your fingers to the screen and show her."

Maisie's cheeks dimpled. "Oh, no. My mommy's coming today. I heard Nana talking to her last night on the phone. And Nana said she'd pick her up at the airport *today*."

"Today?" A handful of bobby pins clattered to the floor and scattered in every direction. Wasn't it only yesterday that Adrienne was nicely situated thousands of miles away across an ocean?

At once, Maisie dropped to her knees and retrieved the pins. "Uh-huh. I think it's supposed to be a surprise because Christmas Eve is almost here."

Did Wes know about the surprise visit? If so, he didn't mention it. Given his history of withholding information, what was another hidden detail? Either way, a little girl stood in front of her, overjoyed at the prospect of seeing her mother. "I'd love to paint your nails." Her forced smile must have appeared genuine because a delighted Maisie skipped off to the polishes. Scarlett swallowed hard and struggled to get a grip. She'd bumped into a…a…well, he wasn't even an old boyfriend. She'd bumped into someone she'd liked, and they shared a few more laughs. Tomorrow morning, she'd be checked out and on her way home. No need to dwell on irrational fantasies.

Chapter Seven

One by one, Scarlett finished each hairstyle. She painted Maisie's nails, cleaned up, closed the salon, and dropped off the little girl with Lucy. Barely enough time remained to regroup for a precious few minutes in her room. Once she cleared her head, she could tend to her own hair and makeup before helping Clarice get ready. As she neared the stairs, a fluttering flared in her stomach. Vivian approached with a woman bearing a strong resemblance to Maisie.

"Scarlett, I've heard you worked some magic this morning. I hope Maisie was more help than harm." Vivian patted the mystery woman's arm. "This is Adrienne, Maisie's mother."

"Nice to meet you." Nothing could be further from the truth. Choking on words was a real thing after all. "Your daughter is a sweetheart." Well, that part was at least factual. "Does she know you're here?"

"Not yet." She flashed a smile full of blinding white teeth. "I just arrived. Viv's bringing her up in a few minutes. First, I want to arrange a few early gifts under the tree."

"You're staying here?" Her breath stopped.

The picture-perfect woman adjusted the bag hanging on her shoulder and climbed the stairs. "The Sapphire Room is my home away from home. I could stay with my parents, but I enjoy my privacy."

If she wanted privacy, she should have stayed somewhere other than the room two doors down from Scarlett's. Another perfect day started off with a bang.

"Enjoy the rest of your stay." Adrienne stepped onto the landing, linked her arm through Vivian's, and entered her suite.

In an instant, the good manners drilled into her as a child vanished. Without attempting a polite goodbye, Scarlett plodded the last few steps to her door. Unsteady, she fumbled with the key card.

Colton's door clicked open.

Every muscle in her body stiffened. Mornings didn't get better than this.

"Off to tux up." He sidled up to the room. "I'll see you at the reception if not sooner?"

"I'll be there." A proprietary hand landed on her shoulder. Another smile plastered over gritted teeth. Her face ached in exhaustion from the effort.

Colton headed for the staircase.

Amazing he could be so cocky after making a total fool of himself last night.

He slid a phone from his back pocket. At the same time, a slim wallet fell to the floor.

Her first instinct was to holler after him, but on impulse, she caught herself and waited for him to descend the stairs. She tiptoed down the hall and retrieved the wallet, opened it, and bingo. The key to his room rested in one of the slots. She'd return the items after a bit of investigating. Incriminating evidence must be in his room. With any luck, she'd hit the trifecta and find the bracelet, wallet, and wedding bands.

One quick glimpse up and down the empty hallway provided enough reassurance to let herself into his room.

Ugh. The room reeked of whatever odious cologne he doused himself with, but now was not the time to dwell. Soon enough, he'd notice his wallet missing and return. Sure, he wouldn't have a key, but finding a staff member to let him in wouldn't take long.

The bathroom first? Skip it. Anything stashed in there or under the mattress would be found by a maid. A peek in the dresser drawers revealed a phone book, a pad of paper, an embossed pen, and the Bible. The unlocked suitcase popped open, and a swell of hope plummeted into despair. With each passing minute, her thumping heart threatened to beat out of her chest. At a loss, she gave up, tossed the wallet on the bed, and bolted back to her room, thanking her stars for the empty hallway.

Scarlett slumped back against the closed door and inhaled a long deep breath, held for ten seconds, and released a slow exhale. She repeated the pattern several times until the possibility of hyperventilating passed. Defeated, she flicked her gaze to the clock on the nightstand. Clarice would be looking for a hairdresser sooner than later. Where had the time gone?

****

"Well, this visit was unexpected." Wes leaned back against the dresser in Adrienne's suite. He couldn't decide if being blindsided by her arrival was better or worse than anticipating it. How did she make her first trip home from Europe without breathing a word?

"You never did appreciate surprises." Adrienne smirked, swept her hair into a tousled bun, and tugged on a cardigan.

Wes grinned and hooked both thumbs in his belt loops. "You're one to talk. Your life has always been one giant planner. How'd you pull off a spontaneous international trip with your schedule?"

She gave a half shrug and wrapped her arms around a squealing Maisie for another flurry of cheek kisses. "Vivian helped. That woman can keep a secret like no one else I've ever known."

Maisie giggled and escaped with a final peck on the head.

"When my parents see who turns up on their doorstep for dinner tonight, I can't wait to see their faces." She dropped onto the bed and sighed. "I could sleep for a week though. How's everything going here? I heard a new hairdresser worked with the bridal party this morning."

"Sort of. She's actually a guest." Aware of the flush of heat reddening his face, he adjusted his cufflinks. Scarlett was more than a patron of the manor. She was a ghost from his past pervading his present. Since her arrival, she'd occupied every free thought.

"Maisie tells me she's quite pretty." A smile played on her lips. Silent for a moment, she lowered her gaze. "Teasing. I met her earlier. It's okay to find other women attractive. I don't expect you to pine away. I'd be lying if I didn't admit to meeting some interesting people myself."

She met Scarlett? Asking the questions sitting on the tip of his tongue would only provoke more questions. He observed Maisie, engrossed in the process of sifting through pieces from her new puzzle. Void of any twinges of annoyance or jealousy related to Adrienne's love life, he redirected his focus toward her. "Thank you for making our arrangement almost easy."

"I could say the same to you."

"You absolutely could." He laughed and shook the

paper bag in his hand for effect.

"I need some help over here." Maisie dumped the remaining puzzle pieces out of a box and sprawled on the floor to examine them. "The more the merrier."

With the ice officially broken, he joined his daughter in her struggle to piece together a picture of the Parthenon. Concentrating on the puzzle proved impossible. He needed to find Scarlett and assess the fallout from her unexpected introduction with Adrienne. Soon.

****

As she made her last swipe with lip gloss, Scarlett heard a light knock. She welcomed the intrusion on yet another phantom conversation that entailed ripping into Wes for leading her on. Volleying between things she wanted to say before checking out and words she wished she'd said last night added up to an epic waste of time.

Clarice waited on the other side of the door with a full face of makeup and her hair in a towel.

No matter how many times she'd been told dirty hair was easier to work with than freshly washed, the woman insisted on shampooing and conditioning.

She pranced into the room holding a garment bag. "I had the dresses delivered to my room to save us a trip. Here's yours."

At the mercy of her stepmother's enthusiasm, Scarlett closed the door and watched her shuffle past with the dress. With the same care she'd use to put down an infant, she deposited the gown onto the bed.

"Where do you want me?"

Scarlett pointed toward a stiff wooden chair at the desk. "It won't be comfortable, but it'll do." She'd kept her own hair simple with light waves and small strands secured by decorative pins. Clarice would want something flashier, and she was ready.

"You look lovely, dear. But give me something with a little more pizzazz."

"Will do."

Satisfied after approving a few requested alterations, Clarice left to get dressed.

Half starved due to missing lunch, Scarlett fumbled with the undergarments that accompanied her dress. The few bites of muffin and one strip of bacon were ancient history. She stood before the full-length mirror and twisted left and right; the layers of deep red fabric drifted to the floor. Strapless had been the right choice. Her white shoulders complemented the color of her hair and the dress. Not bad for a few hours of sleep and working all morning.

She'd have to ignore the dark circles under her eyes refusing to absorb any amount of concealer. Still, Wes wouldn't notice. Adrienne was a stunner, even after traveling a bazillion miles. She'd probably never suffered anything less than a flawless complexion every day of her life.

Time to shove aside those thoughts if she wanted the slimmest chance of enjoying herself tonight. Maybe Clarice needed help with her dress. That diversion never failed to consume all her attention. As she stepped into the hallway, she heard a click.

Adrienne's door swung open.

Wes exited with a paper bag in hand.

Was that surprise on his face? Or dread? Her stomach lurched.

"Hey."

"I've got to help Clarice." She turned to leave.

"Wait, I have something for you."

A parting gift? On impulse, she faced him and shot a pointed glare at Adrienne's closed door. "I met her."

"She really pulled a fast one." He hooked a thumb over his shoulder and half smiled. "Maisie's over the moon."

"You didn't know she was coming?" Unconvinced, her voice fell flat.

"My mom did." He bowed his head and tapped the bag against his thigh. "But she was afraid I'd spill the beans. Apparently, I can't keep a secret."

She bit her tongue to refrain from telling him Maisie already heard. A hollow ache settled deep in her stomach. "I'm sure you'll have a wonderful Christmas together."

His eyebrows knotted together. "She's here for Maisie, not me. I mean, yeah, we'll spend the holidays together because we share a daughter, and we want to get along. But we're not testing the old adage 'third time's a charm.' "

Only a special kind of con artist could stand outside his ex-wife's door, say those words, and not mean them.

He held up the brown bag and closed the distance. "For you."

Scarlett took the bag and opened it. Seeing the box of tinsel inside, she cracked a smile. "You did *not* have to do this."

"You're here for one more night. I want your room to be perfect."

The tension exited her body, leaving a lighter-than-air sensation in its place. "You'll have to help me hang it." At risk of revealing a loss of equilibrium, she reentered her room and placed the bag on the dresser.

"I'd be happy to." He followed her inside. "By the way, you look beautiful."

"Thank you. You clean up quite nicely yourself." Clarice was right. He was prettier than her, and he was even prettier than Adrienne. The tuxedo enhanced that fact. "I heard the wedding bands were missing. Any luck finding them?"

His head sagged. "I wish. The best man finally broke the news to the bride and groom. They're not happy, but the show must go on. They're using tinfoil rings for the ceremony until we get the problem straightened out."

"You're kidding." Incapable of picturing Harper with foil wrapped around her finger, Scarlett lifted a hand to her mouth and giggled.

"Nope." He strode over to the bag and removed the box of tinsel. "I could use a distraction."

"Don't you have work to do? The wedding's in a few hours."

He slid the cellophane wrapper off the package. "I delegated a few things so I could carve out an hour to spend with Maisie before she heads to her grandparents' for the rest of the weekend. The schedule was made before I knew Adrienne would be here. She's anxious to get going because her parents still don't know about her surprise visit." He glanced at his watch and lifted a brow. "I have an extra thirty-two minutes before anyone starts looking for me. And that's a conservative estimate. Last I heard, Harper is eating up every second of attention her lady's maids spend doting on her."

"I guess there's no time like the present." She grasped a handful of tinsel and sprinkled strands across the branches.

Wes joined her but used a heavier hand. Within

minutes, he wore more tinsel than the tree. "Do you think a lint roller would help?" The corners of his mouth twitched up.

Scarlett surveyed her dress and then his tuxedo. She pressed her lips together, then laughed. "I don't think tape will be enough." One by one, she pinched the errant tinsel from her dress and deposited a handful of strands onto the dresser. "I think I got everything."

Wes brushed his palms down his jacket. He inched closer and plucked a strand from her hair.

His hand hung in midair before clasping the back of her neck, and his lips found hers in the lightest kiss, stealing her breath. Tapping at the door snapped her into the present, and she stepped back on rubbery legs. "I-I should get that." Clarice, who never seemed to walk anywhere, glided into the room exuding a mock regal air.

"Well, look at you!" She gawked at Wes. "*Mon Dieu! Tu es très beau, mon chéri. Très beau.*"

Seeing Wes's baffled expression, Scarlett arched back and laughed. Clarice spoke without a hint of a French accent and sucked all the charm out of her words. "The manor is going for a Victorian theme, Clarice, not French."

Clarice swatted a hand in the air and wiggled her fingertips. "Oh, pin a rose on your nose. Who made you the expert? Let's go get Graham. I promised I'd walk into the ceremony on his arm."

Laughter and animated voices sounded through closed doors along the length of hallway toward Graham's room.

Clarice sashayed inside to a shower of compliments. She stopped to help him adjust his tie.

Sighing, Colton squeezed past Wes and entered the

room. "This guy is never ready on time, and he's never learned how to tie a tie properly. I should've known better than to rush." He shrugged. "Guess I have time to make a pit stop." Already unzipping his fly, he stalked into the bathroom.

An unidentifiable clattering and a few expletives resonated through the door.

Still grumbling to himself, Colton emerged from the bathroom. "Wes, the toilet won't flush."

"I'll take a quick look."

Graham lunged toward him. "No, don't. It's fine." He clapped him on the back. "We can deal with plumbing hiccups tomorrow. You've got a wedding to put on."

"It'll take two seconds." Despite the truth in Graham's statement, Wes patted his shoulder and brushed past him.

Colton sneered. "This place is falling apart if you ask me. Multiple thefts and a broken commode." He braced an arm above Scarlett's head. "I hope you'll save a few dances for me tonight."

Pinned to the wall, she lurched with an involuntary gag at the stale breath hitting her in the face.

"Whoa."

The confusion in Wes's voice diverted Colton's attention. Scarlett leapt at the opportunity to sidestep him and peeked into the bathroom.

Wes stood with the toilet tank lid in his hand. He plunged a hand inside and extracted one diamond bracelet, a wallet, and two black jewelry boxes.

As the reality of Graham's deception sunk in, Scarlett slowly placed a hand over her open mouth.

Colton leaned over her shoulder and gasped.

"Yikes." He stepped back and raised his hands. "I knew nothing about this little stockpile. I have my grievances, but I don't bite the hand that feeds me."

Wes rushed past him into the hall.

Graham wasn't a match for his youth or speed and surrendered himself instead of attempting to run down the flight of stairs. He sank to the top step.

Scarlett poked her head back into his room. At the sight of Clarice standing alone and bewildered still holding his tie, Scarlett drew a breath and lifted a hand to her cracking heart.

Chapter Eight

Wes sat motionless at his desk. Twenty minutes remained until the wedding march.

Millie McKay paced the length of his office. "He's pulled a lot of shenanigans over the years, but he's really outdone himself this time."

With his head bent, shoulders hunched, and hands clasped between his knees, Graham sat outside the open office door.

"I'm assuming you'll want to contact the police." Wes shot a glance at their culprit—a schoolboy waiting to be reamed out by the principal.

"Absolutely not." She stopped short and snapped. "I don't need this kind of publicity, and neither do you."

With a face that would bring a grizzly bear to its knees, she marched over to his desk. Wes lurched back in his seat. The motion didn't put nearly enough space between them.

"Colton will help him pack and take him home immediately." One bulging vein protruded from her forehead. Leaning forward, she jammed a finger toward him. "Don't you even think about breathing a word of this fiasco to Harper or anyone from the Donovan family. We'll sort out the gory details tomorrow."

"We let them enjoy their day to the fullest. But won't they ask questions about how everything turned up?" The unexpected decision was difficult enough to process without listening to a woman who resembled a pixie swallowed by a giant satin cloud.

Millie smoothed her gown. "Trust me, Harper will be far too busy to want to get involved in this mess. If Seamus presses me, I'll chalk up the recovery of the rings to luck and nudge him back toward his beautiful bride."

The timing was perfect for Millie's plan. By the time she caught up with the best man and handed off the rings, he'd be ready to walk down the aisle. From that moment on, everyone in attendance would be swept up in the festivities. Wes escorted Graham back to his room so he could gather his belongings and hit the road with Colton.

The doting nephew welcomed the change of plans. Minutes later, he stood in the hallway with bags in tow, already on the phone making plans for that night.

Alternating between humming and whistling, Graham puttered about his room and took his sweet time to pack.

Wes leaned on the doorjamb, his gaze following Graham and his mind on Scarlett. He refused to let her slip through his fingers again—at least not without a fight. He needed a plan that didn't involve a long-distance relationship. Uprooting Maisie wasn't an option. But asking Scarlett to move here would be ludicrous. He'd done everything to give her a million reasons to refuse.

****

Scarlett gaped at the bride and struggled to reconcile this regal beauty with her flashy alter ego. Harper McKay Donovan stunned in her wedding gown, eclipsing everyone and everything in the Victorian winter wonderland ballroom. White silk fitted through

210

the waist flowed into a simple train. A lace overlay extended the length of the dress. Sheer lace covered her arms and neck. The rest of the wedding party, although gorgeous, paled in comparison to the bride.

Guests formed a circle around the dance floor to watch several staff members perform the two-step and a waltz, yet heads continued to drift in Harper's direction.

"Is there anything these people can't do?" Clarice's effort to whisper failed and drew a glare from the man standing next to her. "They're actors, waiters, and dancers. I wonder if they sing."

"Probably," Scarlett responded. Her gaze landed on Wes. For a moment, time stood still. A heaviness lodged in her abdomen. Beneath the carefully cultivated public image and exceptional bone structure was a man any woman would be lucky to build a future with.

He stared from across the room.

A pointy elbow jabbed her side. "What was that for?"

"Do you two plan on making googly eyes across the ballroom all night, or will one of you gather the nerve to strike up a conversation?"

A conversation about what? The one thing left to say at this point was goodbye. Sure, if they lived in a fairy tale these rekindled feelings would end in happily ever after. But real life imposed real distance between them. "We're being rude. Stop worrying about me and watch the dancers."

"When you stop watching every move Blondie makes, maybe I'll consider gracing someone else with my romantic expertise."

Easier said than done. Scarlett spent the last two hours distracted by heart-racing thoughts of this afternoon and the sinking realization she'd been fooling herself. Soon enough, he'd have a few minutes to spare, but she hadn't mentally prepared herself for the moment of truth.

After a meal fit for royalty, Scarlett drifted her gaze along the dinner table adorned with strands of holly. Dinner entailed the lavish fanfare one would expect from the upper crust of the late 1800s. Several candelabras stood centered along the length of the table. Menservants clad in crisp, white shirts and black dinner jackets stood at tables or paraded about holding trays. Maids wearing black dresses with white aprons hustled about, depositing and retrieving silver platters. The desired feeling of being dropped into another century surpassed expectations, but decorations, staff, and guests impeded Scarlett's ability to view the entire ballroom while seated.

She sat back, frowned at her untouched sherry cobbler cocktail, and fidgeted with the white lace doily under the china dish garnished with rose petals not daring to wilt on such an occasion.

"Rumor has it your dance card has been freed up for the night." Wes sat in the adjacent empty seat with a wicked grin.

Excitement flooded her veins, extinguishing the ability to put an end to whatever they'd started. "I suppose a few slots opened up, but I'm not moving until you tell me what happened with Graham."

Clarice sniffed and disengaged from the conversation to her right. "Us. If anyone deserves to know what's going on, it's me."

"True." With only rumors to rely on, Scarlett bit her lip. "The last we heard, Mrs. McKay refused to call the police and insisted she'd handle the family matter herself. After the fuss she made? Why?"

Wes shook his head. "Graham said he never intended to keep the stolen items. He'd taken them to irritate his sister, the bride's grandmother. She's a perfectionist who'd driven him crazy most of his life, and he wanted her to experience a series of adverse events beyond her control."

"At the expense of Harper?" Sucking in her cheeks, Clarice gripped Scarlett's arm.

"He wanted to cause a bit of chaos but planned to mail back everything anonymously." Holding up both palms, Wes reared back. "I know his excuse sounds ridiculous, but I believe he was telling the truth. So does Mrs. McKay. She made a snide comment about how she should have known because he'd upset her apple cart on more than one occasion."

Clarice rolled her eyes and sighed. "Well, I don't get it. At all." She waved at a few coworkers beckoning. "But I am not about to let Graham's hijinks ruin my good time. If you'll excuse me, they're playing my song." She wiggled her way onto the dance floor toward her friends.

For several seconds, Wes watched the boogying guests. Then with an unreadable expression, he turned toward Scarlett, removed a small cardboard box from his jacket pocket, and placed it on the table. "For you."

Raising one eyebrow, she opened the lid and found an exquisite, detailed tea cake with one long, satin ribbon exposed. "Dessert hasn't been served yet." A soft pulsing beat began to thud in her ears.

"I know, but I wanted to personally deliver yours." He withdrew the cookie from the box and rested it on her dessert plate. "Pull out your charm."

With three gentle tugs, a silver flower slid out. "If memory serves, this charm represents a blossoming relationship." Her throat tightened. At a loss for words, she clutched the charm to her chest and searched his face for answers.

"Am I asking for too much too late?" Stiffening, he pressed his lips together.

"You don't think a four-hour drive between us is too much?" Though this statement made sense, in her heart, she knew the miles didn't matter. Until now, she hadn't dared believe he might feel the same way.

Again, he dipped a hand into his pocket and held up an intricate bracelet with a silver butterfly charm. "This one signifies new beginnings." The opposite hand took one of hers, flipped it over, and deposited the bracelet into a trembling open palm. "Stay." The muscles working in his face stilled.

Words refused to form. She fidgeted with the pearl choker, suddenly heavy around her neck. "Here? How?" Every nerve tingled with the growing realization he wanted her permanently in Hemlock Bend.

"You don't have a job or even an apartment to go back to." He edged forward and tapped the table with his index finger. "We need a hairdresser, and we have staff quarters."

"What about the woman I filled in for?" Though she knew any rational human being would ridicule her for allowing the conversation to continue, the warming sensation settling around her shoulders overruled their imagined criticism.

"She'll be out of commission for a minimum of three months and understands our need to replace her before she even starts." Disregarding the manor's rules for formal staff attire, he removed his jacket and draped it over the chair.

The joy, excitement, and overall chaos filling the ballroom faded. Scarlett strained to make sense of his words. "So, I'd work and live here?"

"Many of our employees do. Makes for an easy commute. And if you're not handling an event, you'd rent the chair and be free to use the salon at will." He paused and slid his chair closer. "If you're nervous about committing, stay for three months, and then decide. If you choose to leave, we can call Skylar."

Unwanted, imaginary voices of reason insisted on being heard. "I need a steady paycheck, but your offer sounds too good to be true." Beneath a layer of burning hope in her heart lay fear, doubt, and the nearly palpable memory of fierce hurt. But hadn't fate brought them back together?

"I hope you'll stay for more than the job." He removed her fingers from the pearls, engulfed her hands with both of his, and brought them to his lips.

Only a crazy woman would entertain the idea. Still, the heck with second-guessing herself. In this case, playing it safe risked heartbreak far worse than taking a chance. A plan took shape. She'd go home in the morning and spend Christmas Eve and Christmas Day with her family. By December 27th, she'd be packed and driving to New Hampshire just in time for New Year's Eve with Wes.

One by one, the vows she'd made to herself replaced the logistics of her vision. This scenario fit the criteria of the convenient romances she'd sworn to avoid going forward. They'd never ended well. Why should this love story have a different outcome? She raised a finger to silence him. "One request?"

"Name it." With a set jaw, he lifted his chin.

"If I agree, whatever happens with us on a personal level will move slowly. Snail's pace slow." His gaze locked on hers. The burning intensity from those mesmerizing, emerald eyes could melt Antarctica.

"I'll follow your lead. And I understand if you need time to think over my offer." He half smiled and tightened his grip. "I do come as a package deal."

"I should think over every word you've said. A more responsible woman would make a life-changing decision only after careful deliberation." She looped the two ribbons around her finger and dangled the charms between them. "But I've always been a sucker for a pretty package tied up in a bow." Still grinning, his lips crushed down on hers.

Thank you for purchasing
this publication of The Wild Rose Press, Inc.

For questions or more information
contact us at
info@thewildrosepress.com.

The Wild Rose Press, Inc.
www.thewildrosepress.com